Mistake

THE BREAKING THE RULES SERIES
BOOK FOUR

Mandy,

XOXO

K Webster

Editor: Mickey Reed
Cover Designer K Webster
Cover Photo: Dollar Photo Club
Formatting: Champagne Formats

ISBN-13:978-1503274211
ISBN-10:1503274217

The Breaking the Rules Series:
Broken (Book 1) – Available Now!
Wrong (Book 2) – Available Now!
Scarred (Book 3) – Available Now!
Mistake (Book 4) – Available Now!
Crushed (Book 5) – Coming Soon!
Disgrace (Book 6) – Coming Soon

The Vegas Aces Series:
Rock Country (Book 1) – Available Now!
Rock Heart (Book 2) – Available Now!
Rock Bottom (Book 3) – Available Now!
Rock Out (Book 4) – Coming Soon!

Apartment 2B (Standalone Novel) – Available Now!
Love and Law (Standalone Novel) – Available Now!
Moth to a Flame (Standalone Novel) – Available Now!
Letters from Stadil by Anne Jolin and K Webster - Coming Soon!

Dedication

This book is dedicated to you, my husband.
You're my person.

"You'll learn, as you get older, that *rules are made to be broken*. Be bold enough to live life on your terms, and never, ever apologize for it. Go against the grain, refuse to conform, take the road less traveled instead of the well-beaten path. Laugh in the face of adversity, and leap before you look. Dance as though everybody is watching. March to the beat of your own drummer. And stubbornly refuse to fit in."

— Mandy Hale, *The Single Woman: Life, Love, and a Dash of Sass*

Prologue

First day of college…

You were a mistake. That was a constant reminder in my home when I was growing up. Momma took every chance she could to remind me of just that. A mistake for getting pregnant from a loser? A mistake for not getting an abortion or putting me up for adoption?

My entire life has been one big mistake. Every decision I make always ends up being the wrong one.

In high school, when I joined a drama class just because I thought the teacher was hot, that was a mistake. Turns out, I couldn't act and the teacher hated that I was the worst one in the group. Both he and the class took their digs at me daily about how horrible I was. It was a fucking nightmare.

When I decided to get a job at a restaurant waiting tables so I could save to go see Olive in New York, that too was a mistake. After spilling coffee all over three customers in a single day, I was fired. Apparently, I wasn't cut out for that sort of work.

At eighteen, when a fine-ass black man showed up on my door-step offering to whisk me away to New York City so I could model, well… That was a mistake as well. Turns out, my naïve ass moved in with a psychopathic, sadistic shithead who was obsessed with my sister and just using me to get to her. Big mistake. *Huge.*

I'm tired of making mistakes. Once I set my eyes on the handsome investment banker, Trent Sutton, I knew things were going to turn around for me. In an effort to quit making mistakes and make something of myself, I chose to enroll at CUNY and get my bachelor's degree in investment banking. That would get Trent to notice me.

For once, I was going to learn from my mistakes and start making better decisions. Things are going to change. I can feel it.

Chapter ONE

Nearly four years later…

Opal

I've been fucking friend-zoned. Sitting up in my desk chair, I quickly unbutton my top two buttons of my blouse and poke my chest out. The board meeting is about to start, which means Trent should be here any moment. How that man can resist my constant advances is beyond me. I can see the lustful way he appreciates my body, but he never makes a move. It is fucking annoying. Maybe he is waiting for me to get out of college? The worst thought is that maybe he just doesn't find me attractive.

The latter makes me sick to my stomach. I spend several days a week in the gym building my muscle tone, and everything I eat is extremely healthy. I know that he notices my tight curves, but he never even tries to touch me. It drives me crazy.

"You look pretty today," Andi compliments as she comes in with Jackson, who makes a beeline straight for the conference room while she stops at my desk.

Andi is absolutely gorgeous. Her long, platinum-blond hair is forever smoothed to perfection. She always wears sexy, form-fitting suits that accentuate her curves. Jackson, her husband, has a hard time keeping his eyes off of her even to this day. It makes me happy for her but sad that I can't get Trent to lose his measured control for even a second.

"Thanks, doll. Board meeting," I remind her, winking.

She giggles and throws a glance over at the front doors, where a group of men are entering. "If that asshole doesn't notice you today, you need to fucking move on. Seriously, Opal. You're gorgeous, smart, and spicy as hell. You need a man who will fall to his knees and worship you, not one who treats you like a little sister," she sighs.

I frown at her words. Being treated like a little sister is worse than being fucking friend-zoned.

"Gross, Andi! Now go away. He's coming this way," I hiss and wave her away.

She chuckles all the way to her office, earning a glare from me.

"Good morning, Opal. How is your day?" a sexy, familiar, deep voice asks from behind me.

I suppress a shiver and swivel around in my chair to face him. He looks sexy as hell, like usual, in his navy, pinstriped, three-piece suit. His blond hair is perfectly styled, and like always, I have the urge to run my fingers through it and mess it all up. David Beckham has nothing on this man. Blue eyes twinkle at me as his lips curve into a smile. *Those lips.* God, what I could do to those lips.

"Cat got your tongue?" he teases.

Really, this man has no idea how much I want him. My skin burns, but I quickly recover. Not before I appreciatively run my eyes over his overly toned body though.

"Hey, Trent. Things are perfect now," I breathe out suggestively and cock an eyebrow up at him.

His eyes do the thing they always do when I say these things to him—they darken—but only for a moment. I don't miss when they dart down to my fairly exposed chest, but then they are back at mine in a flash.

"Great. We'll chat after the meeting, hon," he says, grinning, before he saunters off to the boardroom.

I admire his ass until he closes the door behind him. Hopping up from my chair, I head to Andi's office to explain in detail the latest encounter. Ever since I began working at Compton Enterprises four years ago, Andi and I have become extremely close. Olive and Pepper have their kids in common, which means they spend a lot of time together doing "mommy" things. Poor Andi and Jackson are still trying to conceive.

"Opal," Bray calls out from his office as I walk by.

Stopping in my tracks, I peek my head in. "What's up, bro?" I ask. And he is my brother in every sense of the word. He rescued me from Drake that night and I will forever be grateful. It was also Bray who treated my sister like nobody ever could—he loves her and my niece, Abby, with such an intensity that it can be felt by all those around them.

"Want to go visit Olive for lunch at the firing range?" he questions.

Typically, we go visit her at least one of the three days she works up there to help Jo. At first, Bray was overly insistent that she didn't need to work. But my sister wouldn't hear any of it. They didn't need the money, so it was more about her getting out and having adult interaction. On many occasions, Jo has tried to sell the business to her but Olive hasn't conceded just yet.

"That sounds great, Bray. Just holler at me when you're ready," I instruct and head next door into Andi's office.

Normally, I wouldn't bust into her office. I know that Jackson could be ravishing her on the other side. But since I know he is in the conference room, things are safe. When I walk in, I am about to start whining about Trent, but I realize she is crying. Quickly, I close the door behind me and rush to her side.

"Andi, what's going on?" I ask softly as I stroke her hair.

She quickly dabs her eyes and looks up at me. Gone is the playful, happy friend. The girl staring at me harbors a sadness that guts her to her very core. "Oh, Opal, I'm just devastated," she sniffles.

I hug her tight before moving back to the other side of her desk and sitting down. "About what?" I ask. But I know what she's about to say before she even says it. Four years they've been married and she's had five miscarriages.

"It happened again this weekend," she whispers tearfully.

My heart clenches for her. I absolutely hate this for her. She's such a kind, wonderful person who deserves a baby so much.

"I'm so sorry, Andi. Is there anything I can do?"

She wipes her nose and then sets to shredding the tissues anxiously. I have a feeling there's more than the miscarriage going on right now.

"Jackson and I are going back to counseling this week. We've been arguing so much lately. When we have sex, it's so calculated and timed with my ovulation calendar. There's no more spontaneity. Jackson is patient, but I can see him faltering. He never says a word, but I know he resents me for this. I honestly don't know what to do, so that's why I set up an appointment with Dr. Sweeney. Jackson was pissed but never disagreed. Opal, I'm just so miserable," she confesses.

My heart aches for her. "Andi, have you thought about other options? Have you tried in vitro fertilization? Have you looked into adoption?"

She reaches into her purse and pulls out a card. "I actually have an appointment this week to talk to this Dr. Ellis about our options. He comes highly recommended and is really good at what he does. If this doesn't work, I'll look into adoption. I can't take any more of these miscarriages. They gut me, Opal. I'm an emotional mess afterwards."

"Things are going to work out, Andi. Just hang in there. You know I'm always here for you," I remind her.

She nods and attempts a smile. "Thanks, girl. Now tell me about Trent," she demands, changing the subject. "Does he want to have wild sex with you in the conference room?" Her eyebrows bounce suggestively at me.

"I wish, but he doesn't seem remotely interested. I swear, I feel like I'm in high school again, desperately crushing over someone unattainable like my drama teacher," I grumble.

Her eyes widen and she giggles, her low moment from earlier dissipating. "Why does that not surprise me, Opal? Why don't you let me fix you up with someone? I'm sorry, but Trent is just taking too fucking long. When was the last time you got laid?" she questions.

"Drake. He was my first and my last. My fucking vibrator broke from overuse too!" I exclaim. "I'm ready for things to turn around."

"Oh my God. I know what I'm getting you for a graduation present," she laughs.

I cock an eyebrow at her as I stand. "I'd prefer to have the real thing. If you can somehow manage to package up a vibrating Trent, I'm pretty sure you'd be my favorite person ever."

"I'm your favorite person ever anyway."

"True, but I think you better work on that present or else Jackson will take your place as my favorite," I joke.

She rolls her eyes. "As if!"

Laughing, I make my way over to her and give her a hug before heading back to my desk. Then I bury myself in my work until the conference room door opens and the board members file out. Trent saunters back over to my desk and sets his briefcase down.

"How were finals? I forgot to ask and I've been wondering since you were especially having trouble in your international investments class," he says, sitting on the edge of the desk.

My eyes trail up his muscular legs for a second before I make eye contact. "It was a fuck—" I begin but stop myself. He always frowns when I cuss, so I start again. "It was a nightmare, but I passed with a low B. I'll be graduating in a couple of weeks and will be ready to unleash my investment knowledge on the world," I laugh.

His eyes study my face for a moment like he's seeing me for the first time. As he watches me, my heart pounds wildly in my chest. Not wanting to break the spell of him finally noticing me, I drop my eyes to my lap. I gasp when his large hand reaches over and sweeps a strand of hair from my face. Everything in this moment is very still. The temperature of my body feels as if it's risen ten degrees. I've waited a very long time to feel this way.

My eyes finally dart to his, and I feel my panties dampen as I try not to inhale his unique scent. He's regarding me differently for once. I'm not sure I can handle the things he is doing to my heart and mind. Crazy things.

"Well, I think that calls for a celebratory dinner. Would you let me take you to dinner tonight?" he asks in that sexy, deep voice of his.

My heart is on overdrive now. He's never once asked me out. I'm almost at a loss for words. Almost.

"Sure, Trent. I would love to have dinner with you. And dessert too," I suggest.

His eyes fall to my chest but quickly drag back to meet mine. This time, he licks his lips, and now, I know I'll need a panty change.

"Here's my card. Text me your address. I'll pick you up at seven," he says hoarsely and tosses his card on my desk. Then he quickly hops off the desk, grabs his briefcase, and stalks out the front door.

I have a date with the successful, sexy Trent Sutton. I've only waited four years for this day to come.

Chapter TWO

Opal

As Bray and I walk into the firing range at lunch time with our bags of food in tow, Olive is helping a man at the counter. His shirt says NYPD on the back, and it stretches nicely over his broad back. He is obviously a cop, and from behind, he's a hottie. When Olive glances up and sees us, she grins. The man in front of her is bent over, completing his form, so she points at him and mouths, "Isn't he cute?"

Bray grunts and stalks around to the other side of the counter to kiss her neck and whisper something in her ear, which produces a fit of giggles from Olive. I'm pretty sure he is claiming his woman in front of the officer. While I am grinning stupidly at their exchange, the man turns around to see who is behind him. He is a good-looking black man—with his hair cut short and piercing, brown eyes. When he smiles at me, he flashes his perfect, white teeth.

A normal woman would take the opportunity to flirt with such a handsome man. Not me. My heart is already set on someone. I've worked hard for four years attempting to get Trent to notice me and I am not about to mess that up now. We are going on our first date tonight and I couldn't be happier.

I am saved by the ring of my cell phone. Fishing it from my pocket, I wave to him before taking the call outside. I don't recognize the number, but I will do anything to avoid talking to the man inside.

"Hello?" I ask breathlessly.

"Hi, Opal. It's me, Trent. I hope I'm not bothering you," he says smoothly. The sound of his voice right in my ear sends a shockwave of desire right to my core.

"Hi! Everything okay?" I question, secretly praying he isn't calling to cancel our date.

"It's great. I just wanted to tell you to dress up. I'm taking you somewhere fancy," he replies.

"Um, sure," I say. I want to keep talking to him but don't know what else to say.

He's silent for a moment on the other line. "See you tonight," he finally tells me and then hangs up.

Why are things suddenly awkward? This is all I've ever wanted for four years. It is time to put my game face on. *No more mistakes.*

I am admiring my body in this black, form-fitting dress when someone knocks at the front door. After work, I not only bought a new outfit, but also spent an obscene amount of time on my hair and makeup. Everything is as perfect as it can get. The scoop neck of the dress gives a classy view of my cleavage. My dark-chocolate skin is smooth and glistening, and I am proud of my shimmering lotion that makes me subtly sparkle.

After hurrying over to the door and opening it, I break into a huge grin when I see a very sexy Trent on the other side, holding a bouquet of flowers.

"Opal, you look nice. These are for you," he beams as I take the flowers from him.

"They smell amazing! Thank you, Trent. Let me put them in some water and then we can go." I smile and head to the kitchen.

He follows behind me and I quietly sigh at the notion of Trent being in my apartment. My body feels warm with him in such close proximity.

I toss the flowers into a vase and fill it with water. He must have walked closer to me, because after I set the vase down and turn around, our chests nearly touch.

"Oh," I gasp.

He is staring at me with a look I've never seen on him before—a look of want. His eyes appreciatively skirt down my body and I suppress a shiver of being on display for his visual tasting. After his eyes finally skim back up to mine, I nearly melt in the entryway from the heated look on his face.

Tonight, things are going to get hot.

When his head dips down to mine, my eyes flutter closed. Finally, I can kiss the man that's starred in plenty of my wet dreams. But when those full, hot lips of his press against my forehead, I exhale in disappointment.

Chill out, Opal. At least we are making progress.

"Come on. We'll be late if we don't leave soon," he says and takes hold of my hand, pulling me from the kitchen.

There is something stirring inside me. For the first time in the last four years, I doubt the level of interest I have in him. Hopefully this date will end with him finally giving me the kiss I've always wanted. If not, I will be really worried about my sanity.

Trent holds on to my hand until we make it downstairs to the parking garage. When we get to his car, he releases my hand to hold open the door in a very gentlemanly manner.

"Thank you," I say, and he winks, effectively sending a chill through my body. Why did I think even for a second that I was losing interest? He is smoking hot and I most definitely want him any way I can have him.

"So, what are you going to do once you graduate?" he asks as he maneuvers the car out of the garage and down the street.

"Jordan actually offered me a job in the accounting department. I accepted and will begin my new position in a month," I tell him proudly. Even though I'll miss working with Andi every day, I am excited to put my degree to use.

"Sounds like you have it all planned out, Opal. I'll miss seeing you on board days since you'll be hiding out behind closed doors."

Talk is simple and light the entire way to the restaurant. Easy, even. I knew we'd be a perfect match once he gave me the time of day.

After a fairly short drive, we arrive at a very modern, swanky restaurant. He pulls the car under an awning and quickly steps out, handing his keys over to the valet in the process. Seconds later, he opens my door and offers his strong hand. I try not to burst into flames when my clammy hand is enveloped by his burning one. Everything about this man is hot. As he helps me out of the car, he flashes me a grin that effectively causes my heart and panties to catch fire.

Shit, he's so freaking hot.

Once I've stepped out of the car, he places that same warm hand on the small of my back and guides me into the restaurant. The warmth he delivers does nothing to calm the shivers running through my body. *Shivers of need.* Since he already called in a reservation, we are immediately seated at a table in a quiet section of the restaurant.

"So, Trent, we've known each other going on four years now, but I know so little about you. Tell me something interesting," I say.

"There's not much to know. I work alongside my dad at the investment firm. He's grooming me to take it over when he retires in a few years. My favorite thing to do in my spare time is to swim. I was a swimming champ in high school and at college. During the summers, I would lifeguard at the YMCA."

He pauses his story so we can give the waiter our drink order and then continues on. "I also volunteer as a Big Brother. There are so many kids in this city who need a good role model in their lives. It's really quite fulfilling. What about you, Opal?" he asks.

"Well, wow. How do I even top that? Besides, you know a lot about me already," I say.

We're interrupted once again when the waiter pours our wine and takes our food order.

"Tell me more about your job you accepted?" he asks as he sips his wine.

I can't help but admire the way his lips hug the glass. I feel warm and have to refrain from fanning myself.

"Jordan offered me a job as a payroll administrator. It comes with a much larger salary than the one I make now as his assistant. I really love working there, so I of course accepted the offer," I explain.

"You know your degree would be put to much better use at our firm. I could match whatever he's paying if you were ever interested. Of course, he would beat my ass, but he'd also get over it," he teases and throws a wink my way.

A shiver ripples down my body. This time, I actually do fan myself. Does this man have any idea the effect he has on me?

"Thanks, Trent. That's lovely of you, but at this time, I will have to pass. I feel like I'll be at this company for the long haul." I guzzle down my wine before throwing another question at him. "So, do you have any siblings?" Without even trying, he melts my insides and this wine is doing nothing to cool me off.

His brows furrow at my question and he looks slightly angry. "I have one brother and he's a fucking loser," he growls. The tone he used is so different than anything I've ever heard from him, so I'm taken aback. For some reason though, I can't leave well enough alone.

"Why? What makes you say that?" I ask, completely intrigued.

"He's a selfish, self-centered son of a bitch and I don't want to talk about him. What do you do for fun?" he asks in an attempt to change the subject to safer topics.

His question stumps me. What do I do for fun?

I go to school, work, and spend time with Olive and sweet Abby. But what else do I do?

For me?

"I, uh… For fun—" I start but am thankfully interrupted by the ringing of his cell.

"Hello? Good evening, Mother. My day is great. Yes. I see," he says quietly.

I try to focus on my wine glass so it doesn't seem like I'm listening in on their conversation. When the waiter brings us our food, I thank him as I wait patiently for Trent to end his call before diving in.

"Yes, Mother. That was a woman's voice. No, no. Just a *friend*," he tells her.

My heart aches at the idea of still being in the friend zone. Before I can fret about it too much, he continues.

"Yes, I'll ask her, but I'm sure she'll be busy with classes and whatnot. Okay. Talk soon," he says finally and hangs up. "I apologize for that. It was my mother. She wants to know if you would like to come over for dinner tomorrow night. I'm sure you're busy and—" he rattles off, but I interrupt him.

"I'd love to," I smile.

"All right. Well, that settles it, then," he grins and picks up his fork.

As we fall into silence while we eat, I can't help but feel weird about everything. Here I've waited four years for an opportunity for him to even notice me, and when I think he does, he refers to me as just a *friend.*

Will he ever think of me as more?

After dinner, he takes me back to my apartment and walks me up. I can tell he's going to leave once I make it in safely.

"I had a nice time." I turn to face him with my back at my door. God, he looks good enough to eat. "Just text me what time you'll pick me up tomorrow."

My arms are around his waist in the next moment and I squeeze his muscled body in a hug. When I start to pull away, he leans forward and pecks my forehead. This is the second time I received a friendly kiss tonight. But I can't wait any longer for the real thing. Bringing my hands up to both his cheeks, I haul his lips to mine and kiss him softly. His hands make their way to my back, just above my hips, and when I coax open his mouth, his tongue meets mine.

He tastes like wine from dinner, and it's delicious. I want nothing more than to taste him all night long, but he suddenly pulls away from our kiss and steps away from me.

"I should go," he mumbles out and throws a wave in my direction before hurrying down the hallway.

Tears well up in my eyes, but I blink them back. Wooing the man of my dreams is hard fucking work. I know he'll be worth it in the end, but until then, it sucks.

Chapter THREE

Thad

I pull my duffel bag over my shoulder and take one last look at what's been my home the past two months. My new roommate, Jake, checked in two days ago and is detoxing bad. He seems like a cool guy, but I'm not sticking around any longer. They'll take care of him just like they took care of me.

Two months ago, I was a barreling along in life without a care in the world. Sure, I had plenty to stress and obsess about, but my daily regimen of Xanax and Jack Daniel's cocktails melted away all of my worries.

I exhale sharply as I realize I'm about to head right back into the source of my problems. But I'm sixty days sober now and have had some great support, which means I can do this. I have my first appointment set up with a therapist this week too. That should help me stay on track.

While in rehab, my mother visited me every Saturday—her hair perfectly swept from her face and neck into a neat bun, wearing a pressed business suit, with judgmental grey eyes pinning me in my chair from over her glasses. She is the opposite of the typical mother figure. I love her, but we're just so different. I've never measured up to her standards—unlike my perfect older brother. But at least she visited me. My brother and Dad seemed to have forgotten I was a part of the family.

My brother set the example I was supposed to follow. He was the school's best swimmer in high school and also one of the smartest at his school. When he went on to college—*Princeton no less*—he excelled there as well. My parents think he can do no wrong. And it's true. I'll never measure up to him. He will eventually take over my dad's company, but I couldn't care less.

"Be good, Thad," one of the nurses named Tamika teases as I walk past her.

Throwing her a wink and a smirk, I tease her back. "Me? Good? Never, Tamika." With one final wave, I step out of the building and into the warmth of an unusually hot New York spring.

The taxi I called is waiting at the curb. Minutes later, I'm watching everything go by in a blur as I mentally prepare for what's to come once I reach my destination. The trip only takes a few minutes, much to my dismay, and I soon find myself standing at the front door of my parents' expensive townhouse.

In a normal family, it wouldn't be necessary to knock for a visit to see your parents. Not in my family. My family is far from normal. Mom is a Stepford-wife-meets-Cruella-de-Vil. Dad is Mom's puppet—always going with the flow and doing what he's told. My brother is the Golden Child. I think his teeth even flash when he smiles because they're just as fucking perfect as he is.

I knock three times and inhale a deep, cleansing breath. I'll only stay here until I get back on my feet. It isn't a permanent solution in my life, thank God. I try to swallow down the heavy feeling of dread as I wait to be greeted. Finally after a few agonizing moments, the door opens and my parents' butler, Broderick, answers the door.

"Mr. Sutton, we've been expecting you. Please come in, sir," he greets me professionally. Everyone always has to be so fucking perfect in my mother's presence—*even the damn butler*.

"Thanks, Brod," I sigh as I hand over my duffel bag to his waiting hands.

"Sir, please let me show you to your room. Dr. Sutton had the room readied for your arrival so you will feel more at home. Dinner will be served at seven this evening, so feel free to enjoy some downtime until then," he says as I follow him down the hallway to my room.

When we make it to my childhood bedroom, he gestures me inside. I step inside and roll my eyes. Mom changed the décor again, and it seems like something straight out of a designer magazine. It must have cost a fortune to redecorate it like this. And even though she spent all that money to make it look fucking perfect, it still feels impersonal and cold—much like her.

He sets the bag on the bed. Before he leaves, he gives me one more message. "Dr. Sutton says dinner is dressy. She's had some things pressed for you, which are hanging in the closet."

I haven't been here five minutes and already my muscles are tensing up. I sure as fuck hope I didn't waste two months in rehab to mess it all up with one visit to my parents' house.

Once I've shed my holey jeans and T-shirt, I make my way into the adjoining bathroom and take in my appearance in the mirror. I look like shit. My light-brown hair is poking out in every which direction. Dark circles are prominent under my eyes. No trace of happiness or humor shows upon my features. I look so...*empty.*

After a long, steamy shower, I crawl into my bed and push away thoughts of the impending awkward dinner with my family.

Chapter FOUR

Opal

I have a little bit of time to kill before Trent picks me up for dinner tonight, so I thought I would check in with my sister, Olive.

"Have you talked to Momma?" I question hesitantly after some small talk. Olive and I have always been close—and Momma is typically one of our subjects of conversation on our daily talks. It usually ends with me angry and moving on to happier subjects, like Trent.

"I'm trying to talk her into coming for a visit. She's never even met Abby. It would be nice if my daughter could know both of her grandmas. I know that, if Momma would spend a little time with her, she'd be wrapped around Abby's little finger just like everyone else," she chuckles.

I smile when I hear my niece singing her ABCs in the background. For a four-year-old, she is extremely intelligent. The little girl has it all—brains and beauty. She's quite adorable with her light-brown skin, pale eyes, and brown hair. Bray and Olive broke the mold when they made Abby.

"Ugh! Remind me to be busy that day," I groan as I thumb through an interior decorating magazine. I must have ten different subscriptions of these magazines. I'm also quite obsessed with those home decorating shows on HGTV and record them all. Even though my education is in finance, my heart aches to design. While I can dream all day about becoming an interior designer, I know it is nothing more than a hobby. I'll always crunch numbers to make ends meet.

"Opal," Olive chides, "you need to talk to her. I know you're still angry with her for how she's been our whole lives, but at some point, you have to forgive and move on."

"That's just it. I want to move on—far away from her. Did you forget how horrible she's always been to us? I'm sorry, but it isn't that easy for me, Olive. I just can't forget my past nightmares and forge ahead like you do. To me, everything in my past is a lesson of what not to do in the future," I explain.

Olive and I go round and round about this topic. She's so easygoing compared to me. I can't forgive and forget. I just can't.

She sighs heavily, letting me know she's annoyed with my answer, but thankfully changes the subject. "So, dinner tonight with Trent? And meeting the parents?" she asks excitedly.

The smile on my lips is immediate. "Yes. I am really nervous, but I'm also thrilled that we're finally taking a step past friendship. I wonder why he's waited all these years to show any interest. Do you think it was because he saw me as young and, now that I'm graduating, I'm finally dateable?" I question.

"That's probably it, Opal. You're a beautiful, bright, young woman. I think he'd be stupid not to pursue you, especially now. With Bray, he fought hard for us as a couple. We had the odds stacked against us, but he didn't care. To him, I was worth the fight," she sighs happily into the phone.

My heart clenches in jealousy. I love my sister dearly, and I am extremely happy that she has a perfect family. However, I can't help but wonder why I haven't found my happiness yet. Then I hear the doorbell chime and grin. My happiness just arrived, and hopefully, he's here to stay.

"Olive, I have to go. Trent's here. I'll call you tomorrow. Give baby girl kisses from Aunt Opie," I blurt out quickly and hang up.

Hurrying to the door, I worry about my outfit. For some reason, I feel as if I'm going to a job interview. Butterflies are swarming in my belly, making me feel slightly nauseated. Thankfully, I dressed in a serious outfit today at work and opted to wear that to the dinner.

I open the front door and grin at the handsome man before me. Trent looks sexy as hell in his tan suit, which hugs every curve of his muscles and begs to be torn from his body. My skirt is a tight pencil style, making my thighs press together, which is a good thing while I drink in his appearance.

"Opal, you look lovely this evening. Are you ready?" he asks and leans in to peck me on the forehead.

Every time he does that, I feel like a child. What's wrong with my lips?

"I'm looking forward to it," I smile and grab hold of his hand.

We make our way down to the parking garage, and he once again opens the car door like a gentleman. Moments later, we are zipping through traffic to his parents' house. Conversation is light as we talk about the sudden recent downward shift of the stock market and some new trending mutual funds. This is our common bond, and I try desperately to seem educated and well versed on the subject of investments. He seems pleased with my ability to keep up in the conversation. I mentally high-five myself for a great start to the evening.

"We're here," he says in his smooth voice that does things to my insides. I have the desire to fan myself but refrain.

The townhome is stunning and looks quite expensive. I'm still admiring the beauty of it as I step out the car. Trent's large hand splays across my back as he leads me up the steps to the gorgeous, red front door. I'm completely enamored with their home.

"My parents are the greatest. Mom is so supportive, and Dad is a great role model. I just know you'll love them," he grins.

The pride he has for his parents melts my heart. I have anything but for my own mother and don't even know my father. Smiling, I allow myself to dream of a future where his parents are my parents as well. In this fantasy, we bless them with many grandchildren.

My thoughts are interrupted when Trent knocks on the door.

Who knocks on the door at their parents' house?

An older gentleman wearing a black suit and bow tie opens the door. He must be Trent's father even though they look nothing alike. My hands shake with nerves but finally I straighten my back. Sucking in a calming breath, I smile and extend my hand out in greeting.

"Mr. Sutton, it's to meet you. I'm Opal," I say in my most charming voice.

A smile tugs at the corner of his lips when he glances over at Trent as he shakes my hand.

"Um, Opal. That's the butler, Broderick," Trent exhales sharply.

My stomach takes a nosedive to the floor. I'm horrified. "Oh, I'm so sorry." It's all I can manage to get out as we are ushered inside. My skin is crawling as all self-confidence leaps out the window to an untimely death.

"Opal, Trent," Broderick greets as he leads us into a sitting room, "Mr. and Dr. Sutton are waiting for you in the parlor."

Upon arrival at the parlor—*whatever the fuck that is*—I see an older woman with graying hair pulled tight into a bun lift her eyes from her wine glass and pin me with her glare. I shiver from the intensity of it and am forced to look away. On the sofa sits a distinguished man with an iPad in his lap. He must be the *real* Mr. Sutton.

"Mom, Dad," Trent acknowledges and saunters over to his mother.

Her glare turns into a look of joy as she hugs her son. The mother-and-son embrace tugs at my heart because it is not something I shared often with my own mother. When they pull apart, her hard gaze is back upon me as she sizes me up. I try not to flinch, but I can feel her analyzing everything from my skin color, my age, and my outfit choice.

"Mom, this is my *friend*, Opal," Trent introduces. This time, I actually do wince at his chosen word for our relationship.

"Lovely to meet you, Coral," she replies coolly, a smirk tugging at her lips.

In this moment, I realize the woman has decided that she doesn't like me. I could almost scream in frustration. Four years of trying to make something happen with Trent only for his mother to hate me for no fucking reason.

"It's *Opal,* and it's nice to meet you as well, Dr. Sutton," I speak evenly. I meet her glare this time. Just as Bray fought for Olive, I'll fight for Trent and our white picket fence.

Mr. Sutton stands and makes his way over to us. "I'm Trent Senior, but everyone just calls me TS." He smiles warmly and stretches out his hand in greeting.

I relax a bit and shake his hand. "Nice to meet you, sir," I politely reply.

"Well, Trent, won't you and your *friend* join us in the dining room," Dr. Sutton instructs snootily, choosing to emphasize the word friend.

We all begin to leave the parlor for the dining room when a deep voice speaks up behind me.

"So, Trent, if she's just a *friend*, you won't mind me asking her out, will you?" the velvety voice questions.

Trent and I both whirl around to see an extremely good-looking man standing in the doorway with arms crossed. He's wearing an un-buttoned dress shirt over a Nine Inch Nails T-shirt and has paired it with what looks like the holiest pair of jeans he could find. The black Doc Martens on his feet complete the badass, doesn't-fit-in-the-per-fect-home appearance.

"You're back," Trent growls at him. He seems angry at this man's sudden appearance. By the looks of it, he must be his brother.

Against my mind's wishes, my eyes hungrily take in the man's appearance. He seems out of place standing in the doorway of the pristine parlor. His hair is styled in a 'just fucked' sort of way, which makes my hands twitch at my sides with the need to run my fingers through it. Amused, green eyes peer back at me, clearly catching me eyeballing him. I try to look away, but I can't until I've looked over every inch of him.

"You know you missed me, big brother," the man teases, but there is a hint of something in his tone. Bitterness? Anger? Sadness?

"Opal, this is Thaddeus. Thaddeus, this is—" Trent attempts to introduce us, but his brother interrupts him.

"I know, Trent. That's your *friend*, Opal," he replies and meets his brother's glare with one of his own.

The tension is incredibly thick. These two definitely have beef with one another. I shift uncomfortably on my feet. This entire en-counter with his family is awkward, and I'm actually looking forward to leaving, which sucks because I just got here.

Thaddeus strides over to me, so I extend my hand to shake his.

Instead of shaking my hand, though, he pulls me in for a bear hug. I'm almost suffocated by his delicious soapy scent and frantically attempt to refrain from inhaling him. He smells good—too damn good. The way his strong arms hold me in their grip has me feeling slightly weak in the knees. I try to pull away before I completely melt in his arms, but he dips his head to my ear, stopping me with his sensual voice.

"Call me Thad," he whispers, his hot breath tickling the inside of my ear.

I can't help the shudder of excitement that courses through me. With a little pat on my bottom, he releases me—but not from his gaze. No, he greedily drinks up the view of my body—across the swell of my breasts, over my hips, and finally down my bare legs. My skin warms under his appreciative stare.

"To the dining room, shall we?" Dr. Sutton snaps, causing me to jump.

Trent slips an arm around my waist as he guides me into the dining room. My heart thumps, mostly in surprise, at his intimate, possessive touch. Maybe he truly does like me but is a little slow at showing it.

Once we're seated, I nervously place my napkin in my lap. Then I sit up straight and plaster on a smile as Trent takes his seat beside me. Thad has chosen to sit directly across from me, and when I make eye contact with him, my smile falls. His face is serious as he looks me over. Where Trent looks like his father, Thad resembles his mother. But unlike Dr. Sutton's, Thad's face shines with kindness.

His green eyes, so clear and knowing, burrow their way right into my soul. *I like him there.* I greedily take the moment to trail my eyes along his strong, slightly stubbly jawline and I resist the urge to reach across the table to drag my finger along it—just to feel him again. When my eyes find his mouth, I try desperately not to fixate on it— *God his mouth*—the mouth that is now quirking into a crooked grin. Needing to stop looking at it before I embarrass myself, I dart my eyes back to his and he winks at me. *Shit, he knows his effect on me.* My skin blisters under his gaze, and I'm forced to look away before I start fanning myself.

What the hell has gotten into me?

"Maria, go ahead and bring the wine and our salads," Dr. Sutton instructs, interrupting my near meltdown over her son. "Maria is our housekeeper, but she cooks when we have guests over."

I don't know what to say to that, so I glance down at my hands and then back up at Thad. He is pinning me with his heated stare, and I struggle not to squirm. There's something about the way he looks at me that makes me feel desired—wanted, even. *And I hate it.* I'm not supposed to be enjoying the looks of other men while I am trying to woo the one beside me.

As if on cue, Trent reaches into my lap and takes my hand.

Even though I'm willing myself to look everywhere but up at Thad, I can't help myself and give in to glance back over at him. He raises an eyebrow at Trent's hand in mine. I shouldn't feel guilty for this but I do, especially when he slightly shakes his head. My heart sinks—freaking sinks. I swallow down my discomfort as I watch his jaw. Over and over the strong bone clenches and unclenches. He's pissed at me.

Why do I even care what this man I just met thinks?

I force a smile at him and straighten my back. I'm here with Trent. Trent and I are destined to become something. *I think.*

Thad leans back in his chair and crosses his muscular arms over his bulky chest. His eyes never leave mine, and I feel like he's found a way right inside my head. As Dr. Sutton speaks to Trent about something, I steal the opportunity to really focus on the man in front of me. My eyes fall to the neckline of his T-shirt, and a small portion of a tattoo peeks out above it. When I bring my eyes back to his green orbs, he smiles at me again. I can practically hear our nonverbal conversation.

Like what you see?

What? No! I'm here with your brother.

Then why are you checking me out?

I'm not checking you out!

He smirks at me and I glare back at him.

Get out of my head, asshole.

Instead of leaving me alone, he winks at me again. I clench my thighs together. Good Lord, he *has* to stop doing that.

I risk a glance over at Trent. He and his father have launched into a conversation about their work day. I attempt to avoid both the heated glare of Thad and the icy one of Dr. Sutton, who is now showing an interest in our silent exchange.

Thankfully, Maria shows up with a bottle of wine and a tray with salads on it. I feel a small reprieve from their stares as she passes them out and begins going around the table, pouring wine into each glass. When she reaches Thad, she hesitates, but once she sees Dr. Sutton nod her head slightly, she pours his glass.

I furrow my brows in question.

"Maria, I'll take some soda if there is any, or water will be fine too," he says and disgustedly pushes his wine glass away from him.

I don't miss the absolutely furious look he sends his mother. Could things get any more awkward? This whole dinner makes seeing my own mother seem like a cakewalk.

"Thaddeus, darling, one glass is hardly enough to do any damage. Now don't be rude. We have a guest," she purrs in a fake tone.

I see indecision war on his face. He wants to stay here—with me—but he also looks ready to bolt at any second. Finally, he sends an apologetic glance my way, which fills me with panic.

Don't leave. I'm not done looking at you!

Thad throws one last glance in my direction before he stands from the table. My heart pounds because I can see that he's visibly upset.

"If you'll excuse me," he growls and tosses his napkin into his salad. "I'm not hungry." Then he stalks out of the dining room, leaving me all alone with the Big Bad Wolf.

I don't realize I've been holding my breath until I exhale sharply after he's gone.

"So, Opal, is it? Tell me, what is it that you do for a living?" she inquires. Then she sips her wine. The viper's attention is back on me.

I squirm uncomfortably. I definitely feel like I'm at an interview—a test to determine if I'm worthy enough to date her son.

"I'm an assistant at Compton Enterprises, but now that I'm graduating from college, I'll be working in the accounting department," I tell her proudly. I've worked my ass off in school, and I can't help but feel a sense of accomplishment.

"Your master's degree?" she questions snottily before taking another sip of her wine. Her knowing smile tells me that she wants me to feel bad for not having achieved more than what I already have.

"Uh, no. My bachelor's degree," I sigh, defeated.

"Oh, I see." Her condescending tone unnerves me.

I want Trent to help me out of this uncomfortable conversation—to tell me how proud he is of me—but he's in another discussion with his father.

"So, uh, what do you do?" I stammer out. I'm normally a very confident woman, but around Dr. Sutton, I feel inferior and inadequate.

"I'm a partner at a fertility practice. I've been helping families have children for over thirty years now." She smiles, this time a little more genuinely. I can't help but feel even smaller in her presence.

"Wow. That's amazing," I respond honestly. How can I ever measure up to Mrs. Perfection herself?

Thankfully, dinner goes well with polite, although not friendly, conversation. When Bray's mom, Connie, was being a bitch when he and Olive first became a couple, it was easy for me to be able to put her in her place. With Dr. Sutton, however, I am completely intimidated by her cold demeanor and I can't even fathom ever speaking out against her. The woman would fillet me in seconds with her sharp tongue.

When Trent's cell phone goes off, he excuses himself from the table and walks into the kitchen to take the call. All friendly pretenses are gone and Dr. Sutton pins me once again with her menacing stare.

"What are your intentions with my son?" she demands quietly.

I feel punched in the gut but sit straighter in the chair and lift my chin. "I like him and have for some time. It is my hope that we can progress into something more than friendship," I tell her genuinely. An image of Thad pops into my head, but I quickly force it away.

"You're not his type," she bites out at me, her eyes skimming along my arm as I reach for my glass.

I know it's a dig at my skin color, and I instantly hate her for her blatantly old-school way of thinking. Are people really stuck in the 1950s still? How were my sister and Bray able to overcome these ignorant judgments against their union?

"And what exactly is his type?" I ask a little more snippily than I intended to, hastily gulping down some wine to calm my nerves.

She narrows her eyes at me before she speaks. When I glance over at TS, he smiles sympathetically at me but doesn't defend me.

She most definitely wears the pants in this family.

"His type is usually of the blond-haired, blue-eyed variety. Oh, and those who are closer to his age as well," she snaps.

I'm upset with her now, and I can't help but throw back my own snide comment. "Well, Dr. Sutton. You know what they always say— once you go black, you never go ba—" I start to say, but I'm interrupted by Trent as he storms back into the dining room.

"Dad, we need to meet Mohammad Abdul at the office. He's had an emergency and wants to liquidate some investments. I think he's just panicking, but you know he feels more comfortable talking to you," he sighs. "Opal, I'm sorry to cut our dinner short. You're going to have to take a cab home. This is an emergency—one of our biggest clients. I'll call you tomorrow," he grumbles and yanks some money from his wallet.

He tosses the cash onto the table beside me. When his eyes briefly meet mine, he seems to ignore my horrified expression. Without any further words, he and his father hurry out. All I get is a wave over his shoulder as they bustle out. *A fucking wave.*

I'm stung. The smug look on Dr. Sutton's face causes tears to burn my eyes. She knows she's won this round.

"Excuse me. Where can I find the bathroom?" I stammer as I will the tears to stay put until I'm alone. I need to get away—away from her stupid smiling face and the rejection I always feel around Trent. Tonight's let down takes the cake.

"Down the hallway, last door on the left. If you'll excuse me, I'll be retiring upstairs. Just see yourself out. It's always lovely meeting a *friend* of Trent's." She smirks as she stands and leaves me alone in the dining room.

I hate that woman.

The tears begin to roll down my cheeks, so I hurry to the bathroom and shut the door behind me. After walking over to the sink, I put my hands on the counter and look at my reflection. Dark-brown eyes peer sadly back at me. My makeup is streaked from my tears along my cheeks, so I rub them with my palms in an attempt to blend away the mess.

I was pretty enough to model at one time in my life, but apparently, because I don't fit the usual girlfriend material of Trent, I'm just not pretty enough.

I'm pretty enough for Thad...

Squeezing my eyes shut, I try to force out his hungry stare—*hungry for me.*

I open my eyes and reach over to grab some tissues. As I dab at my tears, I try to process how horribly this dinner went tonight. Would I ever catch a break with Trent and finally get to be with him? Do I really want to chase after him if he never intends on being caught?

For once in my life, I'd like to be the one who is being chased—and not by some creepy psycho like Drake who is dead set on getting through me to get to my sister. I want to be the sun and moon for someone.

My thoughts once again drift to Thad. Why I can't get that man out of my head is beyond me. Images of his mouth quirked up into a lopsided grin flood my mind.

The clicking of the doorknob startles me. I'm stunned to see Thad slide inside as if he has every right to be here. He's no longer wearing the dress shirt, and now, my eyes wander over the way the fabric of his T-shirt stretches across his pectoral muscles. My mouth actually waters at the sight.

Stop looking at him like you want to taste him!

"I locked the door," I snap angrily. I'm not even angry at him, but I'm furious as hell with myself. Here I am, lusting after the man before me instead of the man who left me here.

Trent left me here—to fend for myself. Not even *friends* do that to one another.

"And I unlocked it," Thad replies matter-of-factly. Once he locks the door behind him, he walks over to where he's just inches from me.

I'm trying not to notice the concern that's written all over his face. Light-brown brows are furrowed as his green eyes search mine. His soft-looking lips form a worried line, and I instantly miss the smile from earlier.

I blink back more tears but defiantly hold my chin up as I wait for what he has to say. But instead of saying anything, he brushes some hair from my face and grazes my cheek in the process. The intimate touch from him sends a shiver through my body—the second time that's happened. Why in the fuck does my traitorous body react to him

28

this way?

"You have the most striking brown eyes I've ever seen on a woman. They're so expressive—I can see your emotions," he whispers, dragging a thumb over my bottom lip. "And right now, I see that you're affected by me."

My heart is beating rapidly and my breaths quicken at his proximity.

"Thank you, but I—" I murmur, but his thumb presses against my lips, hushing me.

"And your lips." His eyes drop down to my mouth, and he slips his thumb away so he can properly inspect them. "I can't fucking stop looking at these lips. If you were my girl, I'd spend an entire night worshipping them with my mouth until they were swollen and sore."

My breaths are coming out ragged now. Especially when he steps closer to me, which makes me back up until my ass hits the counter. *Shit, I've got nowhere else to run.* But do I want to run? I think he and I both know the answer to that one. His advances don't stop until he's pressed his body flush against mine and I am trapped. Now, I officially cannot breath. Time could freeze in this moment or the world could end, but there's no place I would rather be than feeling him against me, so manly and solid. His smell alone has seeped its way into my lungs and I'm one hundred percent enraptured. And, I can feel his very obvious erection pressing into my belly, which causes my mind to drift to how big it must be based on how it's poking into me. I'm in fucking trouble—and for once, I don't care.

"Thad," I exhale heavily and blink my eyes as to clear the fog I'm in. A normal person would push away the advances of the brother of the man she thinks she is in love with. Apparently, I'm far from normal because I feel spellbound in his presence and I'm not making any moves to escape him.

A small gasp rushes out of me when his large, powerful hands slide to my neck and he rubs his thumbs along my jawline. The way he touches me is so reverent. It's like I'm an exquisite piece of art simply here for his personal viewing. I can't say that I don't like it—because I do. *A lot.*

"I'm going to kiss you now, O," he informs me as his mouth slowly descends upon mine.

Every hair on my body prickles with anticipation. I don't answer him one way or another whether the kiss is okay. Instead, I close my eyes and part my lips for him. My heart thumps in my chest as I secretly enjoy the nickname he just gave me. Seconds later, his warm lips meet mine and he lazily tastes me.

And a tasting is what I would classify this kiss as. His lips softly suck my bottom one into his mouth before he samples my tongue as well. I'm completely wrapped up in the deliciousness that's him.

When a quiet moan escapes me, he kisses me harder—more hungrily and less hesitantly. I whimper again, but this time, I take my turn to explore him with my tongue. He tastes like toothpaste, and I can't help but wonder if he had intentions of kissing me before he came in here. My thoughts are dragged back to the present as one of his hands slides around from my neck down to the curve of my ass. With a squeeze, he pulls me closer to him.

"He doesn't deserve you," he groans in between kisses.

I start to protest, but when one of his hands finds my breast through my blouse, I sigh in defeat. My hands, which I've tried desperately to keep firmly planted on the counter behind me, take on life as they travel up his solid biceps and over his shoulders.

"You like that, don't you, sweet girl?" he growls and nips my bottom lip.

I can feel my pelvis physically aching. I want more—*need* more—from him. I don't know what's gotten into me, but in this moment, I crave the man who's kissing me. When his fingers set to undoing the buttons on my blouse, I don't stop him. I can't stop him when he's expertly kissing me like he owns my mouth. Within seconds, he's pulling my shirt down my arms and tossing it to the floor.

Breaking our kiss, he leans back to appreciate my breasts, which are spilling over my black lace bra. "Holy shit, you're a damn knockout," he praises.

I eat up all of his words. Every single one of them.

He cups my breasts through my bra and intensely studies my face. My chest rises up and down with each needy, ragged breath I take. I can't believe I'm allowing this to progress. Clearly, I am after his brother, but something about the way he looks at me changes the whole game. He makes me only have eyes for him. At least in this moment. In this moment, I want him and him only. And I need him *now*.

Chapter FIVE

Thad

An hour ago, I was heading to the dining room to have dinner with my family when I saw the most beautiful woman standing in the parlor, looking very intimidated by my mother. My brother always seems to get hottest chicks, but this woman was stunning. Tall, probably nearing six feet, she still only came to Trent's shoulders. Her smart pencil skirt hugged her curvaceous ass, and I wanted nothing more than to squeeze it with both hands. I settled for just a swat to it instead.

Her dark skin appeared to be silky smooth on her legs, and I could envision licking her from her ankles all the way to her sweet spot, which inevitably hid between her thighs. Her black shirt was unbuttoned just enough to reveal cleavage from her voluptuous breasts. But those lips. Her lips were my undoing. The moment I laid eyes on her plump pout, I knew I had to have her.

My asshole brother introduced her as his "friend," and while I inwardly celebrated at this revelation, I felt sick when she looked like she might cry. If I had seen her first, I would have claimed her as my woman on the spot.

But now that we just shared an intense kiss and she's staring up at me with hungry, questioning eyes, I'm ready to claim her now.

"God, you are so gorgeous. I want you so fucking badly," I reveal as I slide my hands to her back and unhook her bra. Gently, I pull it away from her body and drop it to the floor. Her fingers grip my hair the moment I suck one of her nipples into my mouth.

"Thad," she gasps and tugs at my hair.

Hearing my name on her lips intensifies my need to be inside her. My cock wholeheartedly agrees as it pushes painfully against my denim jeans through my boxers. God, I need her so badly. I wrench myself away from her and yank off my shirt in an effort to get this party started. Her eyes widen as she admires my sculpted, tattooed chest and tentatively touches me. Goddammit, if she keeps looking at me that way, I'm going to blow my load before I even get my dick out of my pants.

"I need to fuck you. Now," I growl before I once again suck her bottom lip between my teeth.

Screwing some woman in the bathroom of my parents' house when I just met her tonight should seem like a bad idea, especially considering I'm fresh out of rehab and said woman arrived on the arm of my asshole brother, but right now, it seems like a fucking fantastic idea. I break away to look down at my very willing-looking partner in crime. Goddamn, she's hot.

"Do it," she pleads, pinning me with needy, dark-colored eyes.

Without waiting for her to change her mind, I jerk her tight skirt up to her hips. Fucking hell, she's hot with her skirt bunched up at her waist. A tiny pair of black panties is all that is between me and her hot flesh. There's some place I know she'll be even hotter and probably soaked. I slip a hand down inside the scrap of panties and finally feel just how wet I somehow knew she'd be for me.

"Baby, you're dripping for me. Do you want me? I fucking *need* you," I murmur as I push a finger between the lips of her pussy and into her very wet entrance.

"Shit!" she hisses but spreads her legs open so I can gain further access.

All sense of reason flies out the window as I finger-fuck her. Nothing matters but her hot, wet cunt and my fingers diving deeper thrust after thrust. With each caress, she whimpers louder and louder.

Her eyes clamp shut and she drops her head back, revealing her sexy, long neck perfectly ripe for biting. I glance into the mirror and can't help but notice the feral, possessive look in my eyes as I claim this part of her body. Gone is the hollow, empty person—fire now resides behind my green eyes.

"Yes, please," she begs as I bring her closer to the edge.

I snap my attention back down to the woman writhing beneath me and rub my thumb across her clit as my fingers slide in and out of her wetness. Within moments, she's moaning as her orgasm crashes over her. And fuck me, she's hotter than hell as she shudders with each shockwave. Needing her in this moment, now more than ever, I quickly slip my fingers from her and yank a condom from my wallet. After I push my boxers and jeans down, I slide on the protection and tease her pubic bone with the tip of my cock. Her knees are shaking from her orgasm. Before she falls, I trail my palms down to grip her curvy ass and easily lift her slight frame up to set her on the edge of the counter.

"Ready, O?" I ask softly. I don't wait for an answer, though, and slowly push myself into her hot body.

Her nonverbal agreement is to dig her heels into my ass, bringing me closer. Her tight body grips my cock with such perfection that I fight the urge to come right away. My hands find her hips and claw at her as I pound into her hard and fast.

"You feel so fucking good," I groan. Going two months without pussy has left me feeling like a fucking teenager getting laid for the first time. I feel myself reaching closer to my orgasm with each pump into her.

"Kiss me," she begs.

I dip my lips down to brush against hers, but we don't kiss. With each thrust, we breathe our heated passion into each other's mouths. It's hot as hell, but eventually, I can't refrain from her alluring heat and nip her lips with my teeth. Finally, I give in and kiss her hard.

I'm completely fucking hypnotized by her.

My thrusts become rough and uneven as I struggle not to come yet, but when I feel her unravel underneath me, I give in and release my climax. My cock throbs with each burst of my burning, long-overdue orgasm. Once my dick stills within her, I softly peck her warm, wet lips.

"You're amazing, O." I grin down at her after we both stop panting so hard.

She smiles shyly and looks absolutely gorgeous in her post-coitus glow.

"Trent is a fucking idiot for calling you a friend. He's missing out one of the most beautiful women I've ever encountered," I chuckle. But sadly, my words break our spell.

As if she's been doused in ice-cold water, her smile falls and she looks horrified. You'd just think I had asked her if she wanted kill puppies with me or something. With a hiss, she pushes my chest so that we separate and slides off the counter.

"Shit!" she exclaims and quickly sets to cleaning herself up with a hand towel.

"O, listen—" I begin, but she cuts me off. Her eyes are wild as she pins me with her glare. Gone is her passionate gaze—instead, I'm met with a hostile yet contrite one. I feel like a goddamn idiot standing there naked, my pants around my ankles, feeling every bit a fucking fool.

"Don't, Thad. This was a mistake. A big fucking mistake. Dammit!" she snaps as she hurries to put her clothes back on.

Following her lead, I dispose of the condom and yank my jeans and boxers back up.

"I need to call a cab and go," she mumbles, voice shaking.

I want to hug her, tell her that what we just did was not a mistake, that it was fucking amazing. But somehow, I know I need to tread lightly with her. She's freaking the hell out and I'm not ready for her to leave me yet.

"The hell with that. I'm taking you home," I grumble as I pull on my T-shirt.

Tears well up in her eyes and she blinks them away as she exits the bathroom. Once in the hallway, I stalk past her toward the front door. Her heels clack on the hardwoods as she hurries to keep up with me, and she snatches up her purse along the way. On the way out the door, I unhook Dad's keys and lead her out to his Harley. As we reach the bike, she comes screeching to a halt.

"What the hell, Thad? I can't ride on a motorcycle," she whines. "Look at my skirt. There's no way!"

I turn to look at her and can't help the grin that forms on my lips. She looks so fucking adorable all pissed with hands on her hips. If she's pissed now, she's about to become livid.

"We'll just have to fix that, now won't we?" I chuckle as I drop to a knee in front of her.

I hear her breath hitch when I place my palms on her knees and slide them up her thighs. Her body shakes, and no matter how hard I try, I can't lose the stupid smile on my face. She may think this is a mistake, but she sure fucking likes it when I touch her. In a surprise move, I grab the bottom of her skirt with each hand and rip the fabric up nearly to her hip. If I knew it wouldn't piss her off more, I'd run my tongue up her chocolate-colored thigh just to have another taste of her.

"Motherfucker! You just ruined a hundred-dollar skirt!" she snarls furiously and shoves me hard on my shoulders.

I fall on my ass with a thud, my laughter booming out into the evening air. When I look up, my cock thickens and all humor is gone as I stare up at the sexy-ass, angry-as-hell woman standing over me. After recovering from her immobilizing ethereal beauty, I stand up to tower over her and crowd her with my hulking presence. Her fury melts away and her shoulders slump, but she doesn't take her eyes from mine. She wants me—even if she won't admit it. I fucking affect her just like she affects me.

"You can't fight this. Hell, I can't fight this," I tell her softly.

Her lips part, but when I dip to kiss her again, she steps away. "There is no 'this,' Thad." Her comment stings and even she winces from saying it. Confusion is written all over her face.

Fuck my brother—he doesn't deserve her one bit.

"Keep telling yourself that. Eventually, you won't be able to resist me at all," I growl deeply as I wrap an arm around behind her.

She whimpers and her eyes flutter closed again as my face nears hers. I'm just inches from her lips, but instead of kissing her, I unsnap the side bag on the bike and yank out Dad's helmet.

"Put this on."

Her eyes fly open when she realizes I'm not going to kiss her. As I shove the helmet into her hands, I toss her a smug look and her jaw drops in shock. She exhales loudly in annoyance but complies. Once I've stepped around her, I throw my leg over the bike and fire up the loud engine. The explosion of noise echoing down the street causes her to jump, and I laugh, which earns me a glare.

"Get on, O," I instruct, smiling.

When her eyes dart around, I can tell she's nervous about riding. Finally, I see her take a deep breath before she attempts to straddle the bike in the most ladylike way. It's hilarious, so I let out a thunderous laugh. As she positions herself behind me, she punches hard me in the ribs.

"Don't be an asshole," she snaps. Then she rests her hands on the tops of her thighs.

I can tell she doesn't want to touch me. I think we both know that, if she touches me, the fire we shared in the bathroom with flare to life. She'll have fun trying to stay on that way.

"Where do you live?" I question over my shoulder. "And you'll need to hold on unless you want to fall off."

She rattles off her address but doesn't heed my warning about holding on. Shaking my head at her stubbornness, I put the bike in gear and peel out on purpose. Her hands slam around my middle lightning fast, and I chuckle at her obstinate ass. But when she hugs me tighter, pressing her body flush against my back, my humor is replaced by need. I want this woman more than any drug or drop of alcohol I've ever consumed. The desire to consume *her* is a drug in and of itself. I relax and enjoy the feeling of her tits against my back and her arms wrapped snug around me.

As we drive through town, I feel her squirm several times, even lifting herself off the bike. What in the hell is she doing? I realize she tends to do it even more when I accelerate. It doesn't take me long to understand that the vibrations between her legs are probably arousing as hell and she's trying to stop the sensation every time she lifts herself up. A smile tugs at one corner of my lips because this girl, whether she likes it or not, is completely turned on right now.

And what kind of guy would I be if I didn't help a girl out?

At the next stoplight, I reach behind me and grip her hip tight, to hold her where I want her. Her hands fist my shirt as she tries to pull away from me. With my other hand, I rev the engine over and over as we wait for the light to turn. Behind me, she goes batshit crazy and screams at me to let go over the roar of the engine. Her squirms eventually subside as she gives up. Not soon after, I feel her grinding against the seat behind me. It's hot as fuck feeling her writhe in pleasure against me on the bike.

When the light turns green, I accelerate quickly. She clenches my shirt in her fists again and bites my shoulder hard as she finds her release. I groan because now I have a big fucking hard-on and no way of relieving it.

Shit, woman. What in the hell are you doing to me?

I'm not bothered by the fact I'll be suffering from blue balls though. The woman behind me was so wound up from our unexpected union that she needed something to calm her ass down. I smile smugly, knowing I was just the man to do it for her. She appears to be more relaxed and presses her cheek into my back.

There's something about this woman. And holy fuck is she all woman.

I came back home today from rehab with a chip on my shoulder. I was pissed at my parents, pissed at my brother, pissed at the whole damn world. But the moment I laid eyes on this dark-skinned beauty, something lit up inside me and flared to life—something deep inside me that I never knew existed. She started that fire, and I have no intentions of letting her put it out because she thinks we're some sort of fucking mistake.

Fuck that. It's not a mistake. It's fate.

I turn into the parking garage at the building of the address she gave me earlier and park. After I kill the engine, we sit in silence for a brief moment as our ears adjust to the sudden absence of the roar. She's slow to pull away from me but eventually does. Instantly, I miss her warmth.

"I'll walk you up," I tell her after she climbs off and hands me the helmet.

A tiny smile tugs at her lips, but I can tell she's fighting it. I'll bring more smiles to those lips—so many more. She just doesn't know it yet.

"Thad, it's not necessary," she finally responds, feigning assurance, and starts walking toward the elevators. Her hips sway as she attempts to leave me.

Those hips. That ass. *Fuck.*

38

I hop off the bike, ignoring her statement, and saunter after her. "Did you enjoy the ride?" I ask knowingly when I catch up to her.

She presses the call button for the elevator and turns to look at me with wide eyes. "I don't know what you're talking about," she lies.

When the doors open, she rushes inside in an attempt to avoid my blatant statement. With a chuckle, I follow her inside. Quickly, she pushes the button to the fourth floor and stares at the floor.

I fold my arms, lean against the wall, and watch her as we go up. She nervously begins fingering the tear in her skirt and still won't look at me. Her thoughts may as well be on broadcast because I can hear them loud and clear. She hates what she's done. But she also likes it no matter how much she wants to deny it.

I don't know what it is about her, but I want her. Badly. She deserves more than my asshole brother. The emotions that war within her are so clearly painted on her face. She couldn't hide her feelings even if she tried. I can see that she feels something with me, but she's fighting wildly against it. The reason is beyond me. She needs to drop the douchebag already and give me a chance.

The elevator finally opens and she storms out toward the end of the hallway, fishing her keys out of her purse along the way. Once she unlocks the door, she gives me a half wave and hurries inside.

Fuck that!

She's almost closed the door completely when my foot stops it.

"O, you aren't even going to say goodbye?" I'm not going to lie. It stings a little that she is so dismissive after the sexually charged evening we've shared.

The door opens all the way back up and she looks guiltily over at me. "Goodbye, Thad."

Her plump lips have formed a little pout, and once again, I can tell she is fighting between her heart and her mind. I'm going to help sway that goddamn decision. After stalking up to her, I slide my hands up her neck and into her hair, capturing her mouth with mine.

I kiss her hard.

I kiss her with silent words that beg her not to give up what could be.

I kiss her with all the passion and fire I have felt since the moment I laid eyes on this dark-skinned goddess.

39

And then I kiss her softly.

I kiss her gently. *Reverently.*

She deserves to be worshipped with praise and pleasure.

I want to be that man.

She fucking deserves it. We both deserve it.

Through my lips and tongue, I try to convey to her what I feel—how, since the moment I first saw her, she's plagued my every single thought. All thoughts of ridiculously unsupportive families and drug addictions fly out the window. All I see is her. *Opal.*

She moans into my mouth and meets my tongue thrust for thrust. In this moment, all that exists is us and this kiss. But the moment she begins to pull away, I know she'll try to shut me out. Her walls will go back up once and for all.

She finally manages to tear herself away from our kiss and regards me with stormy, dark eyes.

"O." My voice shakes with my plea.

It works because she pauses—she doesn't fully break away from me.

I tug her back to me and rest my forehead against hers. "Trust this, O. Trust that this could be more than what you ever planned for. Trust that we could be something better—something more than you ever imagined for yourself. Don't tell me you can't feel this fire between us." Dipping down, I peck her swollen lips one last time before I reluctantly back away from her.

She looks slightly dazed but attempts to blink back her vulnerability. "I can't." Her statement guts me, but the unsureness on her face gives me hope. She won't get rid of me that easily.

"Let me see your phone," I demand.

She's still reeling from our mind-blowing kiss, but she nods absently as she digs it out of her purse. Once I have her phone in my hands, I quickly text out a message and hand it back to her. Seconds later, my phone chimes.

I pull my phone from my pocket and read the text, feigning shock. "O, you're a naughty girl."

She snaps out of her daze and glares at me when I wink at her. "What did you do?" she questions with a frown before quickly reading the text *she* just sent me.

When her mouth drops open in disbelief, I take my leave.

She's not getting rid of me. Not a chance in hell.

"You're welcome by the way," I laugh as I jog down the hallway, opting for the stairwell, to make my quick escape from the furious woman shooting lasers from her eyes.

Chapter SIX

Opal

My mind is still in a fog from last night. *Last night.*

God, could I have been any more of a whore?!

I was on a date with the man of my dreams and ended up fucking his brother the moment he had to leave me. It was disgusting. *I am disgusting.* Just another big fucking mistake to add to my growing list.

Trent. I feel horrible for what I did. Technically, we aren't dating, and he clarified that by calling me his *friend* on numerous occasions, but that doesn't make me feel any better. I. Want. Trent. Not fucking Thad!

Thad. *God.* That man. He infuriates me. How is it that, with one look, one touch, he has me messing up my carefully laid-out plans?

Thad is a bad boy. It's written all over his handsome face. And he has issues—deep ones—that I am not at all prepared to uncover.

But his lips.

His smell.

His taste.

It's all I can fucking think about and I'm pissed as hell about it.

I'm supposed to be daydreaming about Trent and the future I

know we'll have if I work on him just a bit more. We're a perfect match. He's an investment banker and I'm graduating with a degree in investments. We have so much in common. I can talk stocks and mutual funds until I'm blue in the face. This is something I've perfected over the past four years of dedicated studies. I can't throw all that away after one night.

One seriously fucked-up night.

Why is it that I can't get Thad out of my head? *That kiss.* When he kissed me last night in my apartment, my knees were so weak that I nearly collapsed. I've never been kissed like that before—with such passion.

God, he pisses me off.

Sighing in annoyance, I pull my phone back out and look at the text "I" sent him last night. I try not to smile, but dammit, I'm grinning like an idiot.

```
Me: Thank you for all the fuck-hot
orgasms you gave me tonight. I'll have
wet dreams thinking about your sweet
tongue devouring my pussy. See you soon,
lover boy.
```

I laugh when I realize he's already added himself to my contact list as *Thad In My Pants.* I'm about to slide my phone back into my purse to get some work done when it gets yanked from my hands.

"What the hell?" I hiss and swivel in my chair to gripe at whoever just stole my phone.

"Holy shit, Opal! Who in the hell is Thad In My Pants and why are you talking so dirty to him?" Andi giggles. Her mouth is still open in shock. "Tell me how I did not know about this *lover boy.* Time to spill, girlfriend," she squeals and plops down on the edge of my desk.

I snatch my phone away from her nosy ass and tuck it safely away in my purse. "Andi, it was a mistake," I pout. It's my only answer. God, I don't want to explain this to her.

"Not going to work, hot stuff. I'm not leaving this spot until you tell me how in the hell you've managed to keep a secret lover away from me. When did you meet this guy? Is it serious? I thought you were into Trent," she rushes out. I'm so fucking glad she finds this

43

exciting, because I feel awful about the entire thing.

"Andi, I messed up," I groan and bury my head into my palms.

She lovingly strokes my hair as she waits for me to continue. Andi is my best friend—I won't get away with not telling her the entire story.

"Okay, so, last night, I went to dinner with Trent and met his parents. His mother is a fucking bitch by the way." I look up at Andi and shudder from just thinking about that hag. "Anyway, he kept referring to me as his 'friend,' much to his mother's delight. I felt sick, but what was I to do? In my heart, I know he'll eventually come around. We had even shared a kiss the night before last and it was lovely. But last night. *God.*"

Andi is totally into my story—all she needs is some popcorn and Junior Mints. She patiently waits for me to continue with wide eyes.

"The dinner was a disaster from the moment we got to the front door. I confused his dad with the butler. *Embarrasing.* His mom acted like the Queen of Fucking England and I was a lowly peasant. *Infurating.* And his brother… God, his brother. *Mistake.* Andi, it was awful. I DID something awful," I whine. I bite my lip and look at her as tears fill my eyes. "I ruined everything," I whisper as the tears roll down my cheeks.

"Oh, Opal, I'm sure you're making it out to be worse than it is. What did you do that you think is so bad?" she asks gently.

I laugh bitterly as I swipe at my cheeks with both hands. "I fucked Trent's brother, Thad."

Her jaw drops but the corners of her lips quickly turn into a grin. "Holy shit. Honey, this is great!"

"Great? How?" I demand in disbelief.

"Because, girl, you haven't been laid since you were with Drake and that was hardly what I would call a pleasurable experience. Tell me, did you enjoy it?" Her eyes are twinkling and she's beaming at me.

I just nod my head and let out a wrangled sob.

"Opal, why are you so upset? It sounds like this Thad guy is into you—so much so that you banged him the first time you met him. I'm having trouble seeing the problem," she laughs.

I let out a ragged breath. She has no fucking idea.

"Because, Andi, he's bad news. I can tell by the way his family treats him. Not to mention I am in love with Trent." *I think.* "Trent is my happy ending. Trent is my white picket fence with two point five kids. He's the right choice," I rush out tearfully.

She smiles sympathetically at me and pulls both of my hands into hers. "I want you to listen to me, babe. How did his mother treat you? Like shit, right? Does that mean you're a terrible person? No. So why are you so quick to judge him based on the way they treated him?"

When I frown at her, she continues. "Point made, right? Now, the other thing… I don't quite get why you're so fixated on Trent. I mean, he's nice and successful—and, let's be real, fucking hot. However, he has never treated you anything other than friendly. Opal, I want you to be truly happy, not do what you think seems like the best thing. Sometimes, you have to take a chance on the weird and random. I know I did with Jackson, and it's the best thing that ever happened to me. I mean, he's a Harry Potter nerd and an asshole for crying out loud! But he's my nerdy asshole and I wouldn't trade him in for the world."

We both giggle at her words. Jackson has already told Andi that, whenever they do have a child one day, the baby is going to have a Harry-Potter-themed room. When she turned her nose up to the idea, saying that it wouldn't work for a girl, he promised that they could put Hermione posters up.

"I think you should really be open to whatever Thad might have to offer. And also, start thinking about what you really have in common with Trent besides numbers."

While I mull over her words, she changes the subject.

"Once you dry those tears, come into my office so we can get ready for my meeting with Dr. Martin Ellis. He'll be here in a bit. They're outgrowing their current facility and want to make an offer on a property that we'll redesign the layout for. You're a smart girl, Opal. You'll figure it out. See you in a bit," she chirps before she hops off the desk and strides to the office.

My mind swirls with questions as she walks away.

Should I try something out with a man I've only met once—a sexy, bad boy who drives me borderline crazy because he invades my every thought against my will?

Or should I keep plugging away at something I've been trying to

45

cultivate for four years with a good, solid man who feels like the right choice?

When my phone pings, alerting me to a text message, I pull it out and read it with a smile.

Trent: I'm so sorry about last night. How about a do-over? I'll pick you up tonight and take you somewhere fancy.

When my heart beats happily, I have my answer. I'm going to keep working on my happy ever after with Trent. I just have to figure out a way to push Thad from my head once and for all.

"Hi. I'm looking to meet with Mrs. Compton. I may be here just a few minutes early," a deep, rich voice sounds out behind me.

I swivel in my chair to greet my client. He's an older black gentleman, probably in his mid to late fifties, with slightly graying hair. Other than the gray, he seems to be very fit for his age. His suit is expensive, which is to be expected from a doctor, but his dark-brown eyes are kind and his smile is bright.

"So nice to meet you, Dr. Ellis," I greet him professionally and stand to shake his hand.

When his eyes meet mine, the polite look is replaced by sadness. "Yolanda?" he questions, confusion lacing his voice.

My body tenses at the name—*my mother's name*. He's studying my features as if he knows me.

"No, sir, my name is Opal. Do you know my mother?" I ask.

His eyes widen and he takes a step back. Before he can answer me, Andi comes gliding into the room.

"Dr. Ellis, so glad you made it. Follow me into the conference room and we can go over my proposal," she politely instructs.

He turns to go with her, but not before he throws another glance in my direction, his brows furrowed as in disbelief.

Sitting back down at my desk, I pull out my phone and call Olive. Maybe she knows the man who appears to know our mother.

"Hey, sis," she answers on the second ring.

"Hey! Listen, I have a question. A man came in to meet with Andi and I think he knows Momma. Did you ever know a Dr. Ellis?" I inquire.

"Hmm… Doesn't ring any bells. Maybe it was someone she knew through the church long ago."

I remember the way he looked at me when he thought I was her—with such longing. No, definitely not just an acquaintance. He cared for her in some way.

"I'll try to get more info from Andi later. Do you want to meet me for lunch?" I ask as I scoop up my purse and walk toward the door.

"Of course. I'll meet you at our usual spot. See you soon!"

Chapter SEVEN

Thad

I slept like shit last night. After I came home from dropping off Opal, I lay in bed and thought about our chance encounter all night long. Our connection was instant and scorching. It pisses me off that she feels like what we did was a mistake.

To me, it felt very right.

My life has been a series of fuckups, but now, I am on the road to fix myself. It seems as if Opal were dropped into my lap on purpose, and I'll be damned if I let her go. She shone like a fucking star, and I have to have more of her. Last night was just a taste, a tiny nibble, and it only served as a tease.

I want all of her.

Reaching over, I grab my phone off the nightstand and call my old boss, Griffin.

"Hey, Griff. It's Thad," I greet happily.

Griffin was my brother's best friend in high school. When Griff married his pregnant high school sweetheart, Emma, right after school, he and Trent parted ways. Trent had Princeton and goals of running Dad's company, while Griff went to work doing construction to provide for his new family. The two separated amicably and are friendly if they see each other.

Griff did well for himself over the years. He was a sound businessman, really good at what he did. When the company he worked for was about to go under, he used his savings along with some loans to buy it. Now called GE Construction, the company is one of the most successful construction companies in the city, nailing most of the high-end, bigger projects. Before I went to rehab, I'd been working for Griff as one of his main foremen.

"Well, if it isn't little Thaddeus. How are you doing, man?" he booms into the phone. Booming is the only way to describe his loud, gruff voice. The guy is built like a lumberjack. He even wears fucking flannel and has the burly beard to match.

"I'm doing okay. Just got back from rehab. How are Emma and the girls?" I ask. We haven't talked in months. I miss his hilarious stories about those ornery little rug rats he has.

"No shit, man? That's awesome. Emma's doing great. She just found out last week she's pregnant again. We're hoping to add a boy to the mix. Sasha celebrates her thirteenth birthday next month, and boy, is she moody as hell lately. Lydia is still Daddy's girl and won second place in the fifth-grade spelling bee. And finally, the little monster, Kami… She's just as naughty as ever. Last night, she took a Sharpie to the hardwood floors in the dining room. I thought Emma was going to blow a gasket. When I tried explaining that three-year-olds go through a naughty stage, she got all emotional and worried about giving birth to another 'devil child.'"

We both chuckle before he grows serious again and clears his throat.

"So, what are you doing now that you're out of rehab? You need your old job back? I told you it would be waiting for you when you were ready. And even though you were a hungover asshole most days, you still did twice as good of a job as my main foreman now." He grumbles the last part.

"Really? Thank you, Griff. Congrats on the pregnancy too, man. I was actually hoping I could start soon. I need to get out of my parents' house as quickly as possible. You know what a bitch Mom can be. If I'm going to try to do something with my life, I need to get away from the toxic fuckers in it."

He grunts his agreement. "It's settled, then, Thad. Get your ass up here when you can and I'll put you to work."

For the first time in quite a while, I feel like my life is getting back on track.

Today, Griff and I got right back into the swing of things. I think that, because of our history of being friends for so long there's a trust there that he just doesn't have with his other employees. I would never do anything to jeopardize his business, and he looks after me like a big brother would—*like my big brother should.*

I ended up staying late at work and am in dire need of a fucking shower, but I have to see her again. Before I know it, I'm maneuvering Dad's Harley through traffic toward her building. A few minutes later, I find an empty spot in the garage and then take the elevator to her floor. Once I make it to her door, I can hear Beyoncé's "Single Ladies" playing softly inside. I knock hard so she'll hear me over the music.

"Come on in. I'm almost ready," she calls out from somewhere within the apartment.

Taking her invitation, I let myself inside and close the door behind me.

"I had a wardrobe malfunction. I'll be out in just a second," she promises from her room. Her voice sounds much better than last night. Maybe she's given some thought to my words. I sure as hell hope so.

Walking over to a stack of magazines sitting at her desk, I flip through them. They're all interior decorating magazines. And now that I glance around, I notice that she's cleverly designed her own living space. It's modern with clean lines but splashes of color here and there. Her own space looks just as good, if not better, than the covers of most of the magazines I'm flipping through.

I can hear her singing along to the music and she sounds cute as hell. The smile on my face is unavoidable. Noticing a sketch pad on the desk, I flip through it, being the nosy bastard I am. It's filled with sketches of floor plans, color scheme ideas, websites, and other notes.

I'm about to set it down, but I realize that the music has stopped and she has suddenly appeared in the doorway. At first, her smile is gigantic and I'm mesmerized by how fucking beautiful she is—just like I remember from last night.

Her length, dark hair is pulled up in a sleek bun and pinned all in place. The makeup on her face is heavy, accentuating her full, red lips. A simple pearl necklace adorns her otherwise naked neck. The red dress she's wearing is strapless and knee-length, hugging every delicious curve of her body. Long, chocolate-colored legs stretch all the way down to her very high, black heels. She's a fucking knockout.

"O, you look incredible—like, I fucking can't breathe right now you're so hot. Shit, woman," I growl as I approach her, ready to devour those lips.

Her eyes widen in surprise, but I don't miss the flash of hunger that must match my own look.

"What are you doing in my apartment?" she hisses and takes a step back, crossing her arms over her lovely chest. It's clear she has her fucking wall up.

"You told me to come in. I needed to see you again." I don't stop advancing until I'm inches from her.

She's pissed and it can't be any clearer. But when I lean into her and inhale the intoxicating scent of her perfume, she gasps. When my eyes meet hers, the angry look has dissipated. Indecision crosses her features. Not waiting for permission, I tilt forward and softly press my lips to hers. She's so clean and perfect that I don't want to dirty her up since I still haven't showered.

The way she tastes has been seared into my memory. I take my time exploring her mouth with mine. Knowing that, if I don't quit now, I'll only want more, I decide to break away from our kiss. She surprises me, though. When her delicate hands grasp each side of my face along my jaw, she pulls me closer. This time, she eagerly meets my tongue with hers. Her moan is soft and telling—telling me that she wants me as badly as I want her. Finally, she wrenches away from me, panting, and begins to pace the room nervously.

"Thad, what are you doing here?"

"I told you I came to see you, but clearly, you were expecting someone else." I sound like a fucking pussy, but I'm hurt that she's not all dolled up for me. If I weren't worried about ruining her perfect living room, I'd plant a fist right through the wall—I know exactly who she's all dressed up for.

Last night meant nothing to her.

Her lips form a pout and I can see that she feels guilty. But when her eyes glance over at the front door and then back over at me, I know I've lost.

"Thad," she frowns. She doesn't have to say the words. I already know.

"Have fun with Trent. It looks like he's taking you somewhere special," I mutter angrily. Then I stalk toward the door, eager to get away from her blatant rejection.

"Wait."

With my hand on the doorknob, I turn to regard her with a questioning look. Her eyes are brimming with tears.

"I'm sorry. In another life, Thad. I just can't."

I shake my head in disappointment as I open the door. "Tell me, Opal. Can't or won't?"

She bites her lip but doesn't make a move toward me. Her choice is made.

"There is something there and you goddamn know it." I pause a moment before snapping out the last of my piece. "And you'll realize it when you're with Trent but thinking about me."

Then I storm out the door and slam it behind me. Ignoring the slow-ass elevator, I take the stairs instead, two steps at a time until I make it back to the parking garage.

As I straddle the bike, I try to figure out why the fuck she is wasting her time with my brother. He's never been one to date seriously—*ever*. A few years ago, he dated a chick he looked at differently—like maybe he loved her—but then she was gone. Never has he looked at anyone that way again. *Especially not Opal.* He treats her like she's a fucking colleague and she's too damn blind to notice.

Based on the expression that was on Opal's face, for some unknown reason, she wants to be his main squeeze. She's setting herself up for a broken heart. And the thought of someone, especially my brother, breaking that heart of hers makes me nearly blind with rage.

If she were mine, I'd never break her heart.

Chapter EIGHT

Opal

I blink rapidly to dry my tears the moment he's gone. My heart begs me to go after him, but the sane part of my brain keeps my feet firmly planted in place.

He's right. I can't stop thinking about him.

Not even seconds after he slams the door, I hear a knock.

Thad. He came back.

I'm still frozen in the spot where he left me fighting the urge to chase after him. Pulling myself from my daze, I hurry over to the door and open it. I'm about to throw myself into his arms but stop dead in my tracks.

"Trent?" I mutter under my breath. Even though I knew he was coming, I still didn't expect to see him standing here. I expected Thad.

"Going somewhere in a hurry?" he chuckles.

I'm glad my skin is darker than Olive's because the burning on my cheeks from embarrassment would have given me away otherwise. I flick my eyes down the hallway and my heart sinks when I don't see Thad.

Why did I let him leave?

Trent smiles warmly at me, bringing me back to the present—back to him. What am I doing? Trent was the plan before Thad came bursting into my life. Shit, Trent *is* the plan.

Trent. Is. The. Plan.

"Uh, no. Let me grab my purse," I stutter.

I quickly snatch it off the entryway table and emerge back into the hallway, dragging the door closed behind me and locking it. Now that I've composed myself, I'm ready to face Trent.

Plastering on a winning smile, I ask him, "So, where are we going?"

"I'm taking you to one of the finest steak houses in the city. I promise you'll love it. Oh, you look lovely by the way," he states as he grabs my hand and guides me to the elevator.

Disappointment courses through my veins as I realize I am just "lovely by the way" to him. The look on Thad's face when I saw him moments earlier was of pure appreciation. He wanted me—*needed* me. And I needed him.

Get him out of your head! You need Trent.

The very idea of eating anything right now has me wanting to puke. I hate how Thad left. My heart is bouncing all over the place as I worry for him. He was definitely hurt—that was clearly written all over his face.

Once inside the elevator, Trent leans over and kisses the top of my head. *My fucking head.* I try to keep a proper smile, but it falls away as I think about how terrible a person I am. Is Thad really so bad? He makes me feel things nobody else ever has before. My hand grows cold in Trent's and I feel dizzy.

The elevator opens to the garage level and Trent guides me to his car. Feeling the burn of someone's gaze upon me, I scan the garage with my eyes. In the shadows, they lock on a familiar pair of furious, brooding, green ones. And even though my surroundings spin, he remains steadfast.

Thad.

The breath is knocked from my gut to see him looking all delicious, manly, and still covered in filth as he straddles the Harley. Nothing else exists in the garage but him. However, I'm yanked from my spell when Trent stops in front of the passenger's side of his car.

My gaze briefly flips over to him as he unlocks the car and opens the door for me. When my eyes land back on Thad, he shakes and then bows his head. Even from all the way over here, I can see the way the muscles in his arms tighten over and over again.

I'm sorry.

Tears spring in my eyes as Trent helps me into the car. He's completely oblivious to his wounded brother in the shadows. *I wounded him.* Once seated inside, I quickly swipe away the tears with the back of my hand. I have to pull myself together.

After a few moments, Trent is weaving expertly in and out of traffic toward the restaurant. When we stop at a stoplight, he turns his head and looks at me.

"Listen, Opal, I feel bad about last night. That was rude of me to leave you there at my parents' house with no way to get home."

I know he thinks my mood has something to do with his abandoning me with his evil mother.

Hardly.

I'm upset because I wronged Thad. I know I wronged him. Problem is, I'm not sure how to clean up my mess. I want to be with Trent. Trent has always been the plan. So why do I feel so fucking gutted about leaving Thad in that garage?

"I wasn't being a good *friend*," he sighs when I don't answer him.

That fucking word will be the death of me.

Thankfully the light turns green and he doesn't see me wince at his favorite word.

"It's okay," I manage to sputter out. But it's not okay. None of this is okay.

His hand reaches for mine and squeezes. My skin is clammy and cold. For the rest of the trip to dinner, Trent thumbs the top of my hand while I think about his brother. *Thad was right.*

Dinner has long been over and I've tried to be a witty, intelligent date for Trent, but now, I am exhausted and have taken to guzzling my wine. The challenge has been trying to stay in the present with Trent when my mind keeps replaying every single encounter with Thad.

In another life. God, what sort of bitch am I? Those green eyes of his flashed when I said those words. His eyes asked, *Why not this life?* For four years, I've waited for this moment with Trent, and it's shit. *All of it.* I'm clearly suffering from mental issues, because now that I have what I want, my heart beats for someone else. Maybe I should get Dr. Sweeney's number from Andi.

"Opal," Trent chuckles, interrupting my thoughts, "you should have seen this guy's investment portfolio. It was fucking amazing. He had his hand in just about everything available. When I asked him why he had so many, he very seriously told me he was attempting to *diversify* his assets. The entire thing was ridiculous."

As he continues to laugh, I stare humorously at him. His blue eyes twinkle and his bright smile is perfect. So why do I keep thinking about an angry, green pair of eyes and a lopsided grin. Shaking my head, I drain my wine glass. As soon as it's gone, I stare into it, wishing I had another glass already.

"Hey," he says softly.

I drag my eyes back up to his to find him frowning.

"I'm sorry. I've been talking all night, and you just seem off. Is everything okay?"

No, everything is not *okay.*

"It's fine. I'm just tired." *A lie.*

His eyes skitter down to the small portion of cleavage revealed by my dress, but then they are back on mine. This time, though, the warmness is gone and his eyes are filled with heat. With Trent, I don't see this look often.

"Why don't we go back to my place and watch a movie? You can relax there. I have more wine there, too."

He winks, and I shiver. Everything, from what he's doing and saying, is suggesting something more. Finally. With just one look, he is able to yank me from my thoughts of Thad. This man, *Trent,* is who I want. I've been after him for four years. *Four long years.* The look in his eyes tells me that he's finally ready. I'd be a fool to throw away all of this progress for one person I barely know and stupidly slept with.

I smile over at him. "I'd like that."

I think.

"Welcome to my humble abode," he teases, gesturing into the entry-way of his loft.

The space is absolutely breathtaking. The ceilings are incredibly high. It has an industrial yet modern feel to it. The color scheme is mostly gray, but somehow, it works without feeling cold. The entire length of the loft is lined with large, picturesque windows from floor to ceiling. Those puppies cost a pretty penny for sure.

"This place is amazing—" I start to say but stupidly trip over the area rug due to partly being tipsy and partly these damn heels. My knees hit the carpet hard. "Oh!" I cry out.

In the embarrassing fall, I managed to nick my tongue with my teeth. For some reason, the sting on my tongue and knees coupled with the humiliation I feel causes tears to roll out of my eyes. Tonight is just not my night.

Suddenly, I feel my shoes being removed and strong arms lifting me to my feet. Trent turns me to face him and regards me with tender eyes.

"You're crying."

I nod shamefully.

He lifts my chin and softly presses his lips to mine. The caring move startles me, but my heart begins beating out of control in my chest at our proximity. Just when I think he's really going to kiss me, he pulls away.

I have to stifle the aggravated sigh that tries to rush from my lips. My lips.

"I can't fucking stop looking at these lips. If you were my girl, I'd spend an entire night worshipping them with my mouth until they were swollen and sore."

Why doesn't Trent feel the need to devour my lips like Thad does?

"Make yourself comfortable. I'll go get us something to drink," Trent grins and saunters off to the kitchen.

My mind is all over the place. This is what I want. This is what I have always wanted.

Is it?

Shit!

Thoughts of Thad try and try to niggle their way into my brain and take up residence, but I force them out. I can't make the proper decisions if he's clouding my brain and my judgment.

"Cape Cod?" he asks as he hands me one of the drinks.

"What's in it?" I question, bringing my lips to my glass to taste it. It tastes strong, but I need strong to get over my nerves.

"Vodka and cranberry juice," he winks and sits beside me.

As I did from the wink he gave me earlier, I shiver. Then I take a large sip while he turns on the television. The drink tastes sweeter this time as my mouth adjusts to the vodka.

"What do you want to watch? Thor? The Hunger Games? Wolf of Wall Street?" he asks as he looks through his DVDs.

I don't have to be a rocket scientist to figure out which one he wants to watch. I know my part—the part of me he expects.

"I love me some Leonardo DiCaprio," I grin over at him.

He smiles approvingly at me as he sets up the movie about the financial mogul. Sipping more of my drink, I enjoy the tingling beginning to course through my body.

You wouldn't be wasting time watching movies if Thad were here.

"These drinks are delicious," I babble out nervously as I finish off my glass. Thad was right. Shit!

Laughing at me, he snatches my empty glass and heads off to make another one. He's a little tipsy, therefore he's more relaxed than he's ever been around me. I'm the one who needs to take a chill pill and enjoy this. This has to work. We *will* work. *I think.*

Moments later, he comes back sans his suit jacket and tie. His top two buttons are undone on his dress shirt and he's rolled up his sleeves. He looks incredibly attractive—like the all-American boy next door. I'd be a fool not to think the blond-haired man before me isn't cute.

I'm a fool. He's cute—definitely.

But mouthwatering?

That's what Thad does to me. In fact, just thinking about his stubbly jawline has my body warming all over.

Trent sits beside me, breaking my thoughts from the bad boy on the Harley, and hands over my newly refilled drink. After I take a sip, he leans over and kisses me, this time with a little tongue. I accept his kiss and search desperately within me for the fire—even one little spark. His kiss tells me that he wants more than just that, but I can't help comparing the kiss to Thad's. Thad kisses me with every emotion all rolled into one—*passion, anger, lust, protection*—and I leave the kiss feeling overstimulated in the best possible way. Trent's kiss is just a kiss.

Thad was right.

Trent breaks away with a smile as the movie starts and settles his large hand on my bare thigh. I *wait* for the chills. I *wait* for the butterflies. *Nothing.* Finally, I resolve to *wait* for the movie to begin.

For the next couple of hours, we drink and enjoy the movie. Things are comfortable—dare I say friendly—but not at all what I expected. I expected heat. *Fire.* But what I've gotten is warmth.

Throughout the movie, he kisses me, touches me. I force my heart to comply with his every move. Our bodies *will* learn to be compatible. How could they not? Our minds are certainly compatible. But when the movie finally ends, I'm exhausted from all the forcing. Maybe it's the alcohol, or maybe I'm just tired. Right now, I just want to go home.

"I guess now you'll need to call me a cab. You are in no condition to drive," I sigh with a smile. I had such high hopes for tonight. Things were supposed to be different. We were supposed to work.

He surprises me when he captures my mouth with his again and kisses me deeply. For Trent, this is the most passion I've seen yet. When he pulls at my bottom lip with his teeth, I let out a whimper. Maybe I've been so wrapped up in forcing something that I just needed to give a little more time. The look in his eyes says that he's ready. *Am I?*

"God, Opal, that moan was so sexy. Stay with me. Please," he murmurs against my lips before kissing me again.

His hands find their way to my hips and he hauls me over into his lap. My legs automatically straddle him. His full-on erection pressing into me is a true indication that he's turned on. Does he finally want me after all these years? I get my answer when he shoves my tight dress up over my hips so I can sit on him more comfortably. His kiss becomes more urgent, but my thoughts drift off and I close my eyes.

Emerald eyes glare at me.

I'm sorry.

I blink my eyes back open to get his image out of my head and try to focus on the one in front of me. With each moment that we kiss, he grinds himself harder into me. He definitely wants me. I think I just want to go home.

"Come on. I need to fuck you, Opal," he growls and abruptly stands with me, my legs wrapped around him.

Shit!

I want this.

I want this.

I fucking want this!

"Okay?" It comes out as a question between kisses—a question he answers with more kisses.

With my legs hooked around his hips and his hands on my ass, he awkwardly stumbles as he carries me to his room. Once inside, he breaks our kiss and drops me unceremoniously onto the bed. I snap my eyes shut momentarily. I want this.

"There is something there and you goddamn know it. And you'll realize it when you're with Trent but thinking about me."

My eyes fly back open and I watch Trent as he begins undoing the buttons on his dress shirt. When he slides it away from his perfectly sculpted body, I see that he's free of ink. Thad's contoured chest boasts beautifully colored artistic stories.

I want to know those stories.

Trent unfastens his pants and drops them to his ankles. He winks at me, but all I offer back is a small smile. A forced smile. I observe him nearly fall on his ass as he tries to remove his socks. Eventually, he gives up and leaves them on. When shoves his boxers down, his cock proudly bounces out. I quickly look away from it and down at my legs, which are dangling off his giant bed.

What am I doing?

His dick comes back into view as he stands unsteadily before me. I shudder when he reaches behind me and begins to unzip the back of my dress.

I want this!

Tears sting my eyes when he hauls me to my feet. The dress slides off my body and hits the floor in a crumpled mess at my ankles. My arms hang at my sides, and I choke back a sob as he unfastens my bra. Once it drops beside my dress, I'm in nothing but my panties. Then I wait for the desire to rush through me, the pattering of my heart— anything! Again, nothing. He begins to push down my panties and I step out of them automatically. Maybe my body will suddenly catch fire from his touch.

What the fuck am I doing?

When he gestures to the bed with a smile on his face, I sigh raggedly. Moment of truth. Now or never. So I crawl up onto the bed and lie down on my back.

"You'll realize it when you're with Trent but thinking about me."

Trent retrieves a condom from the bedside table, and I watch as he attempts to sheath himself several times before finally managing to do so properly.

I want this.

I think.

I squeeze my eyes shut and ignore the glaring, green eyes in my head as I feel the bed sink down with Trent's weight. This is finally happening. *Trent.* He spreads my legs apart and nearly smashes me with his body as he collapses onto me. My breath is knocked from me, but I quickly recover. I still can't open my eyes though.

Can't or won't?

I'm not sure what to expect, but what I don't expect is for Trent to grab his dick and push himself inside me. Fuck! The burn of him stretching me without my being aroused takes a few seconds to adjust to. Either he's not too into foreplay or he's just really drunk. Whichever it is, I'm not a fan.

Thad got me off *before* we had sex and it was amazing.

Ah-maz-ing.

"You'll realize it when you're with Trent but thinking about me."

I force myself back into the present and wrench my eyes open. Trent's eyes are closed as his mouth parts open. With a groan, I feel his cock throb within me as he releases his orgasm.

That was it?!

He collapses onto me again and I nearly suffocate from his weight. I'm three seconds from pushing his sweaty body from mine.

"That was so fucking good, baby," he mumbles, his chest still panting.

Good for who?

He slides his dick out of me and rolls off me and onto his back. One more roll and he's on his side, facing away from me. Within seconds, his shoulders rise and fall in a rhythmic pattern. I'm still blinking in shock when he begins to softly snore.

That was it.

Four years, I waited.

And what do I feel?

Regret.

I bite my lip as I realize he is completely passed out. My throat burns as a sob builds in my throat. Tears well in my eyes and silently run down my cheeks.

This was a mistake.

This was *supposed* to be perfect. It was far from it.

Thad was perfect.

I lie there for who knows how long as I quietly bawl my eyes out. Eventually, the crying begins to make me feel queasy.

I'm sorry.

Stumbling naked from the bed, I barrel into the bathroom and barely make it the toilet before I start puking my guts up. I'll never eat steak again. I'll never drink vodka again. And I sure as hell will never even be able to look at Trent again. I heave until my stomach is empty and all I'm doing is sobbing.

This was all a mistake.

Something in my hysterical state possesses me to stagger naked through the loft until I find my purse. Then I fish it out and dial Thad In My Pants.

"You'll realize it when you're with Trent but thinking about me."

"Hello?" Thad answers sleepily.

"I'm sorry." My voice is a whisper—barely audible.

"What?"

"All I do is make fucking mistakes," I slur into the phone.

"Shit, O. What the fuck is going on?" Thad demands. His voice reminds me of thunder, all sleep now gone from it, but it comforts me.

"I'm at Trent's loft and I'm a whore. A stupid woman who does nothing but make one stupid fucking decision after another." Then I start crying again.

"O, stop. You're not a whore." His voice is soft.

I want to believe him. But when I flash back through the evening, I feel sick again. He says something else, but I drop the phone and fly back into the bathroom. Then I puke some more but eventually pass out hugging the commode.

Chapter NINE

Thad

What.

The.

Fuck.

I'm so pissed right now that I'm seeing red. How could that asshole fuck her when he doesn't even like her? She didn't come out and say it, but with all the self-loathing and calling herself a whore, I drew my own conclusions.

Tonight, when I saw her leave with him, it was the first time since rehab that I considered calling my friend Kurt and asking him for some Xanax. Instead, I went home and used my dad's weights to deal with my frustrations. I had just fallen asleep when Opal called me crying from my brother's place.

Unfuckingreal.

After swiping Dad's keys to his Lexus, I slip out of the quiet house and head toward Trent's. I can't believe I'm about to go pick up the woman I like from my brother's house.

What a fucking joke.

Fifteen minutes later, I pull into his parking garage and make my way up to the top floor. The front door is locked, but luckily, since I have Dad's keys, I easily let myself in.

It's eerily quiet, but all the lights are on. Once I storm to my brother's room, I find him passed out on his back, a fucking condom still hanging off his dick.

Motherfucker.

It sickens me, but the need to find Opal overwhelms me. The way her voice sounded on the phone—hollow and empty—I recognized it. I recognized myself in it. Her head is fucked up, and I know fucked up because I am fucked up. And so is she. I'll help her.

When I storm past the bed and into the bathroom, my heart drops into my stomach. Seeing her dark, naked form curled into a fetal position on the bathroom floor is gut wrenching. If the asshole in the other room weren't passed out, I would string him up by his balls and beat the shit out of him.

Why did she have to come here tonight?

Kneeling down in front of her, I softly stroke her cheek with my pinkie finger. She startles and turns her head to look up at me.

Her chocolate eyes are so fucking sad.

"I'm sorry, Thad." Her words are cut off as she chokes out a loud sob.

"Come here, O," I instruct gently. Then I drag her limp body into my lap and embrace her while she cries. With one arm, I hold her to me. My other hand strokes her bare back in a soothing, circular motion.

One of her hands wraps around my middle and squeezes me as if I might suddenly vanish.

"We need to get some clothes on you, and I'll take you home." I want her out of his apartment. It's infuriating as hell trying to soothe the woman you want after she just fucked your brother. I need out of this apartment just as much as she does.

She nods against my neck.

Releasing her, I set her back down on her butt and stand to locate something for her to wear. I stalk back into his room and clench my fists at my sides. He's still fucking snoring in the same position he was a while ago. What a stupid fuck.

I tear my attention from him and start hunting through his dresser drawer, careful not to slam them. If he wakes up, he's getting his ass kicked. So for the sake of his face and my sanity, I need to be quiet. When I finally locate a T-shirt and pair of boxers, I grab them and then stride back into the bathroom. She's still sitting up, but her shoulders are hunched forward and her head hangs shamefully. With a sigh, I kneel back down and push the opening of the shirt over her head. She helps me tuck her arms through the holes. Once her shirt is on, I pull her to her feet, and she holds my shoulders while I assist her in stepping into the boxers. She's shaking like a fucking leaf.

"Hold on," I instruct as I scoop her into my arms.

She hugs herself closer to me as I exit the bathroom. The scent of lavender, *of her*, floods my nostrils. How can someone so flawless like her be as fucked up as I am?

"Where's your stuff, O?" My voice is but a whisper into her hair as I walk past the asshole on the bed and into the living room.

"I just want my purse and phone. I don't care about my clothes," she says quietly as she points to the table where her purse sits.

I place her on the arm of the sofa while I tuck her phone into her purse and then hand it to her. She takes it with quivering hands, so I know she'll never make the walk downstairs. Sliding my arm under her legs, I pick her up again and carry her out the front door, making sure to lock up behind me.

After I get her settled in Dad's car, she immediately curls up in the passenger's seat and falls asleep. I start the engine and begin driving out of the parking garage. While I drive to her place, I can't help but wonder if I'm strong enough to attempt a relationship with this woman. I'm already in a strange place with my own self, but now, I'm throwing everything I have at trying to help her.

Am I making a mistake?

It's already dragging me down mentally and I've only known her two days. What happens if I invest more time in her? Could she be harmful to my recovery?

Twenty minutes later, I'm carrying her sleeping body into her apartment. After shutting the door behind me, I carry her straight into her bathroom and set her on the toilet.

"You should take a bath before you go to bed." My voice is soft but firm. There's no way I'm letting her go to sleep with him all over and inside her. No fucking way.

She nods her agreement but refuses to meet my eyes. While she slowly undresses, I start a hot bath for her. Before it's even done filling, she steps into the tub and sits down. Bringing her knees to her chest, she buries her face in them.

"I'm sorry, Thad," she says again into her legs. "I'm sorry that I always make terrible decisions that impact those around me, you included."

I sit down on the toilet and lean over to stroke her back. "One mistake, Opal."

She shakes her head vehemently. "No, just one *more* to add to my growing list!"

I don't say anything as I begin pulling the pins from her hair. Eventually, the bun falls and long, wavy locks cascade down her back. She's so fucking attractive—even when she's a blubbering mess.

Finally, I speak again. "O, you're talking to the king of mistakes. My life has been one huge fuckup. It's never too late to change. Trust me. I know. I'm two days out of rehab and trying hard not to revert to my old ways. Nobody's perfect, including you. I'll be here for you if you ever want to talk."

She nods her head in agreement. "I'd like that."

I kneel down in front of the bath, pick up the loofa, and fill it with body wash. The floral smell of it causes a half grin to tug at my lips as I realize that it's her body wash that makes her smell so fucking amazing.

"Thad?"

"Hmm?"

"Why'd you go to rehab?"

I sigh from just thinking about the many reasons. "Because I fucked up. I drank like a fish and popped pills like candy. I was nothing but a loser going nowhere. I'd had enough."

She flinches when I begin washing her back but eventually relaxes.

"I'm better now though. I think."

I scrub her shoulders and arms first and then wash around to the front of her legs. Once she stretches them out, I clean the tops of them. Finally, I wash her belly and breasts before rinsing the loofa and hanging it back on the hook. My cock thickens at the sight of her perky tits, but tonight is definitely not the time. Hell, there may never be another time.

"I'll let you finish up in here," I groan as I exit the bathroom, leaving her alone. Then I stride into her room and dig around in her drawers until I find a nightgown and some panties. By the time I return, she has already drained the water and is standing in a towel. "Here are some clothes. I'm going to go grab you some water and ibuprofen. Where do you keep it?"

Her eyes are trained on the floor as she stretches out her hand to take the clothes. "In the cabinet above the refrigerator," she answers. She still won't make eye contact with me and my heart fucking aches.

A girl I've known for only two days is gutting me because she won't even spare me a glance. I rescued her like a knight in fucking shining armor and she can't even look at me. This shit sucks—I'm in fucking deep already.

"I'll be right back," I say gruffly.

When I get to her refrigerator and pull the cabinet above it open, I refrain from yanking it right off its hinges. Inside, beside some pill bottles, a few prescription and a few over-the-counter, are a several bottles of liquor. The combination of it all burrows right inside my head. What kind of pills are they? Vicodin? Xanax? Oxy? With shaky hands, I reach past them and grab the large container of ibuprofen. My fingers brush against a bottle of tequila and I feel burned, causing me to jerk my hand away. I need to get her into bed and then get the fuck out of here before I lose my shit.

I slam the cabinet door shut and locate a bottle of water from the fridge. After I dump some ibuprofen into my hand, I leave the bottle and practically run back to her room. Away from the prescriptions that are begging me to read them—out of curiosity, of course. Once in her room, I find her crawling under her sheets. She settles in before I hand her the water and medicine. After she swallows it down and sets the water on the bedside table, she finally looks at me.

Do I look guilty as fuck? I wasn't going to take any of her pills.

"Listen," she says softly, jerking me from my jittery thoughts, "I don't really have the right to ask you this, but I am going to blame it on my inability to think clearly due to the alcohol. Since it's late, do you just want to stay here tonight? As friends? I just want to be with someone right now. I'm a selfish woman and will be okay if you say no."

Her beautiful, sad, brown eyes are my undoing. But at the same time, they're calming. I go from panic mode about the pills to just wanting to hold her. I would probably give her the entire world if she asked for it.

"Of course," I answer in a rush and raggedly run my hands through my hair. When she smiles, I *know* I'd give her the world if she asked for it. The sexy-ass woman before me is every bit as alluring as the pills to a former junkie. "Let me turn off the lights first."

She nods and curls up under the covers while I run through the apartment shutting off all the lights. When I pass by the kitchen, I stop dead in my tracks. Once again, my eyes flit up to the cabinet above the refrigerator.

I will not look in that cabinet again.

My feet have other plans, though, as they carry me over to it. Reluctantly, I creak the door open. The pill bottles beg me to read them and feed my curiosity. I huff in frustration at my lack of willpower and grab all three pill containers. One is a high-dosage anti-inflammatory. Another is a muscle relaxer. But the last one kills me.

The last one is a painkiller.

Lortabs.

I slowly turn the bottle upside down and then right again. Out of thirty pills, only a few seem to be missing. I look at the date and furrow my eyes at the date. Four years old?

Suddenly, she calls out to me from the other room and I nearly drop the bottle. I quickly push them all back into the cabinet and quietly close it. Striding toward her room, I fish my phone from my pocket and set my alarm clock along the way.

When she sees me appear in her doorway, she smiles in relief.

"What happened four years ago?" I demand a little more harshly than I intended.

Her eyes widen in surprise, but she doesn't answer my question.

"When I was getting your ibuprofen, I noticed some pill bottles dated four years ago. Were you hurt?"

Fear flashes over her features for a moment and my protective instinct flares to life. Something fucking happened.

"Nothing," she squeaks out.

I cock an eyebrow at her and pull off my jeans but leave my T-shirt and boxers on. Her eyes drop to my dick, but she hastily looks back up at me.

"Don't lie," I grumble as I crawl into the bed and under the covers beside her. Wrapping my arms around her, I spoon her from behind, enveloping her with my warmth. The lavender-scented body wash floods me and I inhale her more deeply.

"Another one of my mistakes," she murmurs. "I'll tell you. But not tonight."

In another life?

My thoughts are from obsessing over knowing what the pill bottles are to knowing how she got them prescribed to her in the first place. It almost seems as if she were in some sort of accident or something. When she rests her hand on my arm and soon falls fast asleep, I try to fall asleep as well with this beautiful woman snuggled up against me. Instead, I spend most of the night with wide open eyes and Lortab on my brain.

My internal alarm clock, a.k.a. my dick, wakes me up before my phone alarm does. With Opal pressed against me this morning, my cock is erect and ready to play. *And God how I want to play.* Her supple body begs to be tasted—every fucking inch of it. Too bad I won't get the opportunity today. She feels fucking perfect, all warm and soft... I could spend every morning like this.

Groaning at my inner pussy, I roll away from her and throw on my jeans. She looks stunning as she peacefully sleeps, her dark skin a beautiful contrast against her cream-colored sheets. Knowing she'll feel awkward after last night, I slip out of the apartment before she wakes up.

After a shower and a change of clothes at my parents', I walk into the office to meet up with Griff. He texted me earlier saying that he wanted to talk about something.

"Hey, Thad," he booms from behind his desk as I walk in.

"Hey, Griff. What's up? Already ready to fire my ass?" I tease, grinning. I'm joking, but my nerves are truly on edge. My mind, which I thought was stronger after rehab, seems fucking rattled to the core after last night. With no sleep, I'm feeling tense.

His loud laughter rumbles through his chest as he shakes his head no. It comforts me in some way, but I feel like the proverbial ball will still drop.

"Fuck that, Thad. You are a hard worker. I'm going to let Les continue on as foreman though." His voice is stern—less brotherly and more authoritative.

Shit.

My stomach clenches because I thought, from our conversation yesterday, he was going to put me back in as foreman. But I had left him high and dry while I'd run off to rehab, so it's understandable. I can feel myself getting worked up though, and my thoughts flit to Opal's cabinet. To the painkillers.

What would the pills even do to me after two months of nothing? I'd probably get fucked the hell up.

"Oh, okay, man. No big deal," I lie.

He beams at me and winks, dragging my attention back to him. I'm fucking confused.

"I have something better for you. My friend, Chester, has gone into house flipping. He's recently bought up several properties that need to be gutted and redone. Since I am trying to expand my company, I have partnered up with him. However, obviously, I can't do the work because I need to be here. I need someone I can trust who will get in there and do just as good of a job as I would do. Now, if you're game, I will assign you a crew. You've always had a knack for detail and want things perfect. This would be a great opportunity for you. If you accept, I'll give you fifty percent of my half from Chester as your pay. Additionally, you'll continue on receiving your normal salary. What do you say?"

I'm blown away. This is my chance. I need to shake the funk I'm in so I can move forward in my recovery—with my life. This is an amazing opportunity. I'm fucking pumped! While commercial construction is what I know, he's right. I prefer the smaller, detailed jobs.

House renovations are right up my alley.

"Dude! Are you shitting me? I'm fucking stoked, man. When do I start?" The cheesy-ass grin is on my face before I can stop it.

He chuckles and tosses me a set of keys. "The address is on the key ring. It's a townhouse in a high-end part of town. We'll go over the budget and what Chester would like to see done. He's a pretty easygoing cat, though, and trusts our creative ability. Go give it a look after we talk about what we're working with budget-wise and you can get started. This is your baby, and I know you'll blow me away."

My face hurts from smiling like an idiot. "Thank you—not only for being a great boss and friend, but also for being the big brother Trent never had the balls to be. I'm going to make you proud, man."

"Don't go getting sentimental on my ass," he groans, but his eyes twinkle in amusement.

I finally have something to throw myself into and keep my brain off the toxic things in my life.

Alcohol.

Fucking prescription painkillers.

And Opal?

Chapter TEN

Opal

What is that obnoxious sound that has crawled into my brain and taken up residence? After ignoring the noise over and over again, I finally roll over and realize that it's my phone.

Shit!

Fumbling through my purse on my nightstand, I yank out my phone and notice that I have missed sixteen calls from Andi and it's almost noon. My head pounds furiously in unison with my rapidly beating heart.

Dialing her number right away, I nervously bite my lip. I've never been late or even missed work in the four years I've worked there, but now, I feel like I ruined all that hard work.

She answers on the first ring with a screech. "So help me, Opal! You scared the shit out of me! I am actually two minutes from your apartment. Are you home?" She's pissed and I can't blame her one bit.

"Yeah, I'm here. Bring coffee, babe," I whine before we hang up.

I burst from my room toward the front door and unlock it before hopping in the shower. Knowing that an angry Andi is on her way, I take a quick shower and throw on some slacks and a blouse. No time for pussyfooting around. I've barely managed to pull my hair into a bun and slap on some mascara before I hear her come in.

"Get in here, woman!" she snaps from the other room.

I nervously round the corner and meet her in my living room. Once her furious eyes find mine, her anger melts away as she looks over my appearance with concern.

I flash a fake smile and motion for her to sit on my sofa. But she holds my gaze for a few seconds more as she scrutinizes me before moving to sit down. Finally though, we both plop down side by side and she hands me my coffee. I groan at how delicious it smells and my stomach grumbles it's appreciation as well.

"Okay, Opal. You need to spill it. What the fuck is going on with you? You've been a mess for *two* days now. This is totally not like you and I'm worried sick." The stern tone coming from my sweet friend indicates her concern for my wellbeing.

I groan as I sip my piping-hot coffee. "Andi, I am so stupid. So fucking stupid."

She just arches an eyebrow as she waits impatiently for my story. I can tell she is about two seconds from shaking it out of me, so I hurry and continue.

"Last night, I got invited on a real date with Trent to make up for the night before. I heard a knock on the door and thought it was him. When I walked out of my room, I found Thad standing there, looking hotter than hell, all dirty from his day at work. He looked at me like I was the most beautiful thing that walked the Earth. And then he kissed me. He kissed me with more passion than I've ever been kissed with before," I admit, sighing.

She frowns. "But you had your date still with Trent?"

Nodding, I continue my fucked-up tale. "I asked him to leave and he was barely gone before Trent showed up. Trent's reaction was not what I'd hoped for, but I was geared up for our date. I started getting tipsy during dinner, and Trent asked me to come back to see a movie at his place."

Andi's eyes widen and she asks in a hushed whisper, "Opal, you didn't sleep with him, did you?"

I purse my lips together and give her a slight nod. Her jaw drops but nothing comes out.

"We got pretty wasted and one thing led to the other. Next thing I knew, we had sex and it was a nightmare. I didn't even get off. He practically fell asleep on me after he came. But that isn't the worst of it," I exhale loudly.

"Honestly, I don't know how much worse the night could have gotten," she murmurs in disbelief.

"I got sick a little bit after and decided to call Thad."

"No. Please tell me no," she mutters, shaking her head.

"Yep. Stupid. What do I do? Do I try to keep things going with Trent or try something with Thad? I'm so confused."

"Opal, listen to me. You have messed this up pretty good. I think you need to take a step back and focus on you for a while. You've been so fixated on your goals that you have been whizzing through life. For once, you need to discover who Opal is—not who Opal thinks she *should* be. That means, back away from both men for now. Once you are in a better place, then maybe you can focus on your love life." She's wise for a woman not even thirty years old.

"I think you're right, Andi. I'm sorry I worried you today. Did I miss anything major?" I ask in an attempt to change the subject as I sip my cooling coffee.

"Actually, I was on my way to meet Dr. Ellis at his office. Want to come with me and then we can ride back to work together?" she questions as she stands and straightens her skirt. She's always so impeccably dressed and beautiful. No wonder Jackson adores her. She's also one of the sweetest, most caring people I know—and that's why I adore her.

"Yes. Sounds great. Why are we meeting him? Do you have paperwork for him?" I stand and locate my purse.

"I do, and I actually have an appointment with him, remember?" Her smile is one of pure happiness.

"Oh! Yes! About seeing if you are a good candidate for in vitro?" I'm so thrilled for her.

"Yep. I'm so nervous. I just pray this will work." Tears fill her eyes momentarily, but she quickly wipes them away.

"Andi, it's going to work. What does Jackson think about it all?"

"He just wants me to be happy. And right now, trying this *will* make me happy. You have no idea how hard it is for me to see Pepper and her big, pregnant belly these days. I want—*I need*—to be happy for her, but until I get this sorted out, it is really hard to be the right kind of friend for her. I'm just a mess emotionally."

Walking over to her, I hug her tight. "You'll get through this, babe. We're going to get through this rough patch together."

"How'd it go?" I ask, standing from my chair in the waiting room.

Andi walks over with a huge grin on her face. "According to Dr. Ellis, he thinks we're good to start the process. I have an appointment set up for both Jackson and me to proceed. I'm so excited!" she squeals and hugs me.

We chat for a few more minutes about what she can expect before Dr. Ellis rounds the corner.

"Mrs. Compton, are you ready to meet in my office now?" he questions.

When our eyes meet, the same look of familiarity is in his eyes. He looks me over once more before motioning for us to follow him.

Who is this guy and how does he know my bitch mother?

During the meeting, Andi shows him what he needs to sign and goes over a few documents with him. When we stand to leave, he seems extremely nervous.

"Um, Mrs. Compton, do you think you could let Miss Redding and me speak alone for a moment?" he asks.

My skin goes cold. There is something about him that makes me incredibly uncomfortable—like whatever he wants to talk about will be something I won't want to hear.

Andi nods after she throws a confused glance in my direction. Then she lets herself out.

"Miss Redding, may I ask you a few questions?"

"Please just call me Opal," I tell him firmly and meet his gaze. Holding my chin high, I prepare for whatever questions he has for me. I know they have something to do with my mother, so I steel myself for whatever they may be.

"You look just like her," he begins, and his nervous smile stretches into a fond one.

"Well, you know, she's my mother," I bite out. I don't mean to be rude, but I am ready for him to get to the point.

"And you have her saucy attitude as well," he chuckles, his kind, brown eyes twinkling.

I anxiously fidget in my seat. *Get to the point, old man.*

"I'm sorry, Dr. Ellis. I can see that you knew my mother once upon a time, but Andi and I really must get back to work," I finally huff out and reach for my purse on the floor.

"No! Opal, please wait. Let me tell you a story," he pleads.

The sadness in his eyes forces me to give in and relax back into my chair. Then he shifts nervously in his chair but finally proceeds with his tale.

"During my last year of med school, I was called away to take care of my sick mother. My studies had to be put on hold, and I was devastated on all fronts. Not only was my mother dying from cancer, but the leave would put me behind in school. I was stressed to the max.

"My mother loved to go to the park and watch the kids play. She knew she was dying and would never have the chance to see her own grandkids. Each day after lunch, I'd wheel her down to the park in the neighborhood. One of those days, a beautiful woman and a stunning little girl came to play. The little girl couldn't have been more than two, but she was fascinated by my mother and her wheelchair. Those two became fast friends, and the little girl, Olive was her name, would curl up in my mother's lap and let her hold her—it was as if those two belonged to each other."

Tears fill his eyes, and I exhale the breath I've been holding. The moment he said my sister's name, I became enthralled with his story.

"Yolanda, the little girl's mother, was absolutely gorgeous. Tall, just like you, and had the silkiest dark skin I'd ever seen on a woman. She carried herself with grace and pride. I quickly learned she was a single parent to little Olive. Each day, we'd sit on the park bench and talk about everything while Olive and my mother played. Yolanda knew I was in school to be a doctor. She knew how difficult it was for me to be caring for my dying mother. Our connection was instant, and it didn't take long before Yolanda and Olive were coming over to the house at night, bringing supper, and eventually spending the night.

Olive stayed glued to my mother's side—and I stayed glued to your mother's," he smiles wistfully and winks.

My heart is pounding because Momma never told me of this story. And the Yolanda from his story sounds a lot different than the one I know and have known all my life.

"I'll spare you the details, but Yolanda and I quickly became romantically involved. I loved her early on, pretty much the day I laid eyes on her, and wanted to be the man for her. As my mom's health declined, I realized my time with Yolanda and Olive was also coming to an end. At some point, I would have to make a decision. Either go back to New York and finish school or stay in Detroit with those two girls."

Now, his tears are really falling, and I have the urge to go around the desk and hug him but I don't.

"And then my mother died peacefully one morning. I was devastated, as were Yolanda and Olive. They accompanied me to the funeral and stayed by my side until she was buried. We spent one more night together. I knew in that moment I wanted to have a family more than a career. When I got up the next morning to tell her I'd decided to stay in Detroit, I found a letter. Yolanda told me it was better for me to follow my dreams than to stay with a single mom. She told me in that letter that she didn't want me to resent her one day for being the reason I didn't go after what I truly wanted. Trouble was, she was so wrong. Nothing else mattered except her and that little girl."

His expression is serious—and so sad. I gulp down the emotion choking my throat.

"Why didn't you go after her?" I demand with a wobbly voice. Even I have a big enough heart to feel sorry for the Yolanda in his story.

Squeezing his eyes shut, he shakes his head sadly. "Opal, I did. I looked for them for two weeks while I took care of my mother's affairs. They had moved out of their apartment and were nowhere to be found. I was honestly devastated. Eventually, I had no choice but to come back to New York and finish school—alone."

While his story is sad and I feel bad for him, I still don't know why he's telling me all of this.

"Okay, Dr. Ellis, I am incredibly sorry that my mother broke your

78

heart, but I don't know what you want me to do. My mom is not the same woman you remember. In fact, we don't speak. I'm sure Olive would love to meet with you though. She has a little one of her own now." I smile thinking about little Abby.

"No, Opal. As much as I want to reunite with Yolanda and Olive, that isn't what this is about." He pauses before dropping his bomb. "Opal, I think I may be your father."

My heart stops beating at this point—or at least it feels that way. This man with the kind eyes sitting before me could possibly be my father? I'm dumfounded and in shock.

"I, uh, am not sure—" I stutter but he stops me.

"Honey, I'm a good man. If I am your father, I want to be that person in your life. Had I known Yolanda was pregnant with my child, I would never have let her leave my sight. Would you be willing to do a DNA test? And even if you aren't, I would still love to be a friend to you and your sister. What do you say?" he questions hopefully.

What do I say?

The only thing that feels right.

"Yes."

Chapter ELEVEN

Thad

"I want to add arches to the doorways in the hallway at each end," I tell Manuel, the leader of the crew I've been given.

He points and says some stuff in Spanish to the other crew members, who all nod in understanding. "Okay, Mr. Sutton. From everything you have told me, I think we can have all of the drywall prepped for painting in a few days," he promises and writes something down in his notebook.

"Please call me Thad. And that's great. I want to get through all of the things on my list as quickly as possible. The less time we sit on this property, the better for the investor. I'll let you guys get to work," I tell him and then make my way back into the kitchen.

The kitchen is where I'll be sinking a ton of the budget into. Thankfully, the house has good bones and just needs some cosmetic issues taken care of. The kitchen, on the other hand, needs all new cabinets, appliances, fixtures, and flooring.

I'm jotting ideas down in my notebook when my phone chimes, alerting me to a text.

O: Hi, Thad. Thank you for taking care

of me last night.

I groan at the memory from last night. This thing with Opal is a fucking joke. I really like the girl, but her head is all over the place. In my fragile, post-rehab state, I can't jump into a mess like that without making myself vulnerable again.

Me: It was no problem, although I hope to never do it again.

O: Listen, I really like you. As friends of course. Maybe we could hang out one day and talk?

I want to roll my eyes at the "friends" part. For a chick who hates that fucking word, she seems to use it a lot herself.
Can I allow myself to try a friendship with her?
Do I have that much self-control?
Romantically, we just wouldn't work—especially if she is hung up on my brother. But friends I can do. I certainly don't have many of those.

Me: Okay. Friends, O. Honestly, I could use a real friend.

O: Thank you for giving me a chance, Thad.

I stuff my phone into my pocket and hope I didn't just make a big fucking mistake by agreeing to this.

The rest of the day goes by quickly as I am immersed in the plan of the renovation. Not once do I think about Opal or any of my past vices. I'm pumped to see the finished product of this renovation. I finish by locking up the house, and I'm heading to Dad's Lexus when my phone rings. Seeing that it's Kurt, I hesitate before foolishly answering my best friend's call.

"Thaddeus! My man!" he greets when I answer.

His welcoming voice tugs at something inside of me. He's my best friend and I miss him—drugs or no drugs.

"What's up, Kurt? How are things?" I question as I fall into the driver's seat.

"Dude, things are great. I'm dating this hot-ass chick named Rhonda. Sounds so fucking eighties, but this chick is fine. We're having a get-together tonight. You should stop by."

I wonder why I am even considering his invitation. But I do consider it. Can we hang without me giving in to his easy peer pressure?

"You know, Kurt, it probably isn't a good idea. I'm just back from rehab, man," I groan. Kurt has been my friend since middle school, so it is hard for me to tell him no.

"Thad, I know and I can appreciate you wanting to stay sober. But I really want to just hang out and shoot the shit. I miss you, man. Just come by the apartment. Nobody is going to pressure you to do anything. I just want to catch up," he assures me.

We always have a good time together, but we were also usually high. I still miss my friend though, so I finally give in.

"Okay, but I'm just going to hang out for a bit. Fucking Whitney won't be there, will she?" I growl.

Whitney is my ex-girlfriend who dumped me when I went to rehab. The relationship was a weak one to begin with, but the fact that she had been so quick to get rid of me annoyed the shit out of me.

"No. Now get your ass here and bring pizza. I have the fucking munchies like you wouldn't believe," he laughs and hangs up.

Sighing, I try to ignore the voice of reason in my head telling me that this isn't a good idea and start the car to go see my friend.

"Thaddeus fucking Sutton," Kurt laughs when I walk through the front door of his apartment.

His tall, thin frame saunters over to me and pulls me in for a hug. After he releases me, I set the pizza boxes on the kitchen table.

"Seems longer than two months," I tell him as I hunt for plates. I used to spend most of my free time at his place, so I know where everything is. "Where the fuck are your plates? Did you move them?" I open a fourth cabinet and still can't find what I'm looking for.

"Oh, Rhonda moved shit around. She's been staying here, like, every night, but it's cool. I really like her, man." He moves past me and retrieves some plates from the only cabinet I didn't look in.

I sit down at the table in the kitchen and start dragging gooey, steaming slices of pizza onto my plate. After working my ass off all day with no lunch or breakfast, I'm fucking starved. Kurt pops the cap off a beer he finds in the fridge for himself and sets a Pepsi down in front of me. I exhale in relief that I didn't have to decline his offer for the alcohol. Maybe we can be friends without it impacting my recovery.

We've just started shoveling hot pizza into our mouths when a cute, petite blonde bounces into the kitchen.

"Babe, meet my best friend, Thad," he says, introducing me to her.

I shake her hand and smile. She's pretty but totally high on something. I suppress a groan as I wonder what it is.

"I'm Kurt's girlfriend, Rhonda. He talks about you all the time," she gushes and begins bouncing around the kitchen. The way she flits about makes me wonder what in the hell she's on.

She grabs the counter spray from underneath the sink and begins cleaning the already spotless counters. I'm kind of in awe of her energy.

When I meet Kurt's eyes, he points to his nose and makes a sniffing gesture.

Coke.

"She keeps this place fucking immaculate," he laughs before shoving another huge bite of pizza into his mouth.

I'm trying not to appear uncomfortable, but knowing she's high right now makes me feel uneasy.

"So, are you still working at Louie's garage?" I question after swallowing down a bite.

Kurt is a master when it comes to rebuilding transmissions. Unfortunately, his problem is actually making it to work. Once he's there, he is the best of the best. But his track record for reliability is pretty low.

"Yeah. Rhonda works next door at the diner. She has to be there bright and early, so she gets me up so we can ride together." Over his shoulder, loud enough for her to hear, he adds, "I'm telling you, that girl is marriage material."

She giggles but continues to scrub the fuck out of the sink.

"That's awesome, man. I'm glad things are going so well for you," I tell him honestly. And I am very happy. He and Rhonda seem to have a good thing going.

"Are you back working with Griff?" he probes as he polishes off his pizza.

"Yeah, and he has me heading up a renovation project. If I can do a good job, I could make some pretty good money at it."

He nearly chokes on his pizza laughing, "Like you even need any more money, asshole."

"You know I don't touch her money," I snap and slam my fist on the table.

Holding his hands up in mock surrender, he grins. "Dude, chill out. I was just messing with you."

A knock at the door interrupts our conversation and Rhonda scurries away to answer it. Moments later, after a flurry of female chatter, Rhonda and Whitney walk into the kitchen.

Whitney.

Of course, Whitney looks like a perfect fucking knockout as usual. She's wearing a pair of skinny jeans that hug every inch of her round ass and a tight, pink tank with a low-scooped neck that reveals the tops of her perky tits.

"Well, if it isn't my boyfriend, Thad," she purrs and strolls over to me.

I roll my eyes at Kurt as she comes behind me and wraps her arms around my body. Her nails dig into the flesh on my biceps, and I recall that, not long ago, I enjoyed those damn things when she clawed my back during sex.

"Hey, Whit. I'm not your boyfriend, remember? You broke up with me when I went to rehab," I grumble and try to shake her off of me.

Even though I sound annoyed, it really was for the best. Whitney is one of those toxic people who, if I have any hope of becoming a better person, I'll avoid at all costs. She still hasn't let me go though. No, she brings her lips to my ear instead. Her previously sexy scent just smells like cigarettes and cheap perfume to me now.

"Thad, let's go to my place and I'll show you how much I missed you," she flirts, ignoring my earlier statement, and nips her teeth at my earlobe.

In the past, this sort of behavior would have had me yanking down her jeans and slamming my cock into her right across the kitchen table. It's almost embarrassing how many times Kurt's seen my dick. Whitney and I used to fuck whenever the mood struck—even in front of others.

Pulling away from her grasp, I abruptly stand up, forcing her to step away from me. "It was nice seeing you Whit. And, Kurt, I'll see you again soon. Rhonda, good to meet you. I have an early day tomorrow, so I'm going to head out."

I slip out of the apartment before I get too much of an argument from any of them. I'm really proud that I was able to see my buddy and not have the desire to do anything stupid. Hell, I even saw Whitney and wasn't tempted to get wasted and fuck her until we both passed out like old times.

The trip home is uneventful, but I can feel my anxiety rise as I walk through the front door. I feel her presence. But when I attempt to make a beeline for my room, my mother's voice halts me.

"Thaddeus darling, please come chat with me," she calls from her sitting chair in the living room.

I stifle my groan because I am living under their roof for the time being and don't need to mess that up until I get my own place. After walking over to where she's sitting, I plop down onto the sofa. Once she realizes I'm still in my work clothes and sitting on her expensive sofa, she scrunches up her nose in disgust.

"Hey, Mom. Have a good day?" I inquire. My attempt at small talk is weak. I'm not sure why I even try. She clearly has something to say to me and it isn't a friendly 'how was your day' sort of chat.

She purses her lips together into what she must think is a smile but is really just a grimace. "Yes, *son*. I wondered what your plan was now that you're back home. Do you plan to go back to school? When do you plan on getting your own place? Your father and Trent have already stated that, if you want to go to work for them, they'll find a position for you."

I try hard not to roll my eyes. It would be a cold day in Hell before I would ever work with those two.

"I'm thinking in about a month I'll have enough saved to move out, Mom. Griff has a new project and—"

She waves me quiet. "You have a trust fund, son. Why you never use it is beyond me. Whatever. Very well, then. Thirty days."

I don't know why I'm in shock at her words, but I am. I hardly ever touch the money in my trust fund. And I hate the fact that she thinks money can solve fucking everything. I'm about to storm off to my room, but she stops me with a little shake of her glass. The jingling of the ice gets my attention and I relax back into my seat.

"Friday night is the benefit for the foundation I started. You'll be expected to represent this family. Dress is black tie. Do not show up in one of your ridiculous outfits or you'll be right on the street. I will not tolerate disrespect. Let me know before Friday if you'll be accompanied by a plus-one," she instructs coolly.

I study her face for a moment, trying to remember if there was ever a time that she acted like a real mom and not some Disney villain like Maleficent. The best memory I can conjure up is one from high school.

My favorite class in school is shop, which turned out to be an unexpected surprise. I was supposed to take art, but in a last-minute overfilling of the class, I got switched. At first, I acted very much like the rich boy I am and snubbed my nose at the idea of taking the class. Building shit was something my family paid to have done. However, it only took a couple of days before I was hooked.

Now, here I am, putting the finishing touches on a bookshelf for my mother. I heard her complain to Dad several times that she needed a bookshelf for her medical books. Most books were tall or thick, which meant that the shelf needed to be deeper and sturdier than most. Mom has been searching high and low for exactly what she is looking for. She even mentioned that she wants it in a cherry finish to match the furniture in her office.

I begin stacking all of the books on the shelves and even take a few decorations throughout the house to add to it. My heart starts to race when I hear her heels clicking down the hallway toward her office. Seconds later, she opens the door and, at first, glares at me for being in there. But when her eyes flit over to the bookshelf, they widen in surprise.

"How did your father find exactly what I've been looking for?" she questions in disbelief while she hurries over to it. Her hand slides down the side as she observes the handiwork.

Before I can answer, she's talking again.

"Oh, I see, Thaddeus. Your father had it custom made for me. It's absolutely stunning. He's good to me, you know," she confides with a grin. My mother never smiles like this, so my heart is now pounding with pride.

"Actually, Mother, I made it. Everything I learned in shop class helped create the shelf from start to finish," I tell her proudly.

Instead of pulling me in for a hug, she turns her smile into a frown. "You're no longer in art class?" Her voice has risen a couple of octaves, making all the happiness I feel about the shelf fly out the window.

"No, but I'm in shop class, and it's awesome because—" I begin but am cut off by a wave of her hand.

"I'll go down to the school tomorrow and have it switched back, son. There's no sense in you taking that dirty class." Her tone is cool and mocking. She knows I enjoy the class and is eager to take that away from me.

"Mom, please don't," I beg, but she once again waves me to a halt.

"Darling, we are 'haves.' 'Haves' don't build things—they have them built for them by 'have nots.' Once you accept the fact that you are a 'have' and not a 'have not,' you can enjoy life a little more."

I feel defeated and blink back angry tears that are fighting to surface. Her eyes, in the rarest of occasions, soften their gaze.

"Thaddeus, don't get upset. The shelf looks nice in here. I'm actually quite fond of it."

And with that, my mother turns on her heel and leaves me alone in her office, still reeling from her compliment. My heart thumps against my chest as I bask in her words. Knowing she liked my bookshelf makes the switch back to art class the following day a little easier to bear.

"Thaddeus?" she snaps, jerking me from one of my only happy memories.

"Sorry. What's that?"

"I said that will be all for the evening. Goodnight," she dismisses me.

Rising to my feet, I start to leave, but she holds out her glass, which is still full of amber liquid. My throat squeezes as I realize she's been drinking.

"Thaddeus darling, will you be a dear and run this to the kitchen for me?" Her expression is even, but I've known her long enough to see that she is testing my willpower. Just like last night. Sometimes, I wonder if she feeds on my failures.

Well fuck her. I won't fail.

I clench my teeth and wrap my fingers around the chilled glass, taking it from her. Storming from her presence, I stalk into the kitchen. I'm about to pour it into the sink when I catch a whiff of one of my favorite vices. With my free hand, I clutch the edge of the sink. Bringing the glass to my nose, I inhale the scent. My mouth practically waters as it begs for a taste. Fuck my mother for putting me in this position.

Bringing it from my nose, I hold it over the sink again. My hand shakes as I try to force myself to pour it out. Before I can second-guess my reasons, I put the glass to my lips. I can taste the strong flavor just on the glass, and I want it so badly.

Fuck you, Mom.

Tipping my head back, I allow some of the liquid to pour into my mouth. It burns as I swish it around, not yet giving in to swallowing it. I can spit it all out and not undo two months of rehab. I'm strong than this.

In a dramatic spray, I spew it back into the sink.

I'm stronger than this—stronger than my mother gives me credit for.

So why am I bringing the glass back to my lips?

Why am I once again pouring the liquid into my mouth?

Why am I gulping until there's nothing but ice in glass?

Fuck. Me.

Chapter
TWELVE

Opal

I crawl into bed after a long and confusing day. Waking up late and hungover this morning sucked, but waking up with nothing but Thad's soapy scent left on the pillow beside me was worse. Discovering that Dr. Ellis might be my father was shocking, and my mind is still reeling with the sad story he told me. And when Trent called to apologize for his behavior the night before, I calmly let it go to voicemail. He sounded sincere on the recording, but I wasn't ready to deal with him just yet.

A knock on my door startles me from my thoughts, and I throw on a robe over my pajama pants and camisole. Who would be coming over unannounced this late at night? Peeking through the peephole, I'm pleasantly surprised to see Thad standing on the other side. After unlocking the deadbolt, I open the door to greet him.

"Have you ever heard of something called a phone?" I tease with a giggle. But the moment I speak the words, the laughter dies in my throat as I realize he isn't okay. "Thad, what's wrong?"

He palms his face and then runs his fingers through his hair before looking over at me with his soulful, green eyes—eyes that appear to be outlined in red possibly from crying.

"What did you do?" I question softly as I step into the hallway and envelop him in a hug.

The moment we touch, I feel the tension leave his body. My heart swells that I'm helping him with whatever's going on in his head. With everything he helped me with last night, I'm glad to repay the favor. I bury my head into his chest and rub his back. Then his hands find my hair and tangle themselves in it.

"I fucked up, O," he exhales in a rush. His tone is full of self-hatred, and it sickens me that he feels this way.

"Honey, we all fuck up. It's a part of life. I'm sure whatever it is can be fixed. Come inside so we can talk about it," I instruct and begin to pull away.

He squeezes me tighter to him, almost to the point where I have trouble breathing. Finally, though, he releases his grip and kisses the top of my head. But his kisses, unlike Trent's, are reverent and alive.

Taking hold of his hand, I guide him into my apartment and lock it up behind me. All the lights are off, so I guide him to my room, where the light is still on. He pauses briefly to glance over toward the kitchen but then allows me to pull him into my bedroom. When we reach the bed, I let go of his hand and he kicks off his shoes before climbing onto it. Falling face-first onto my pillow, he lies quietly for a minute. Then I drop the robe, following him, and sit with my legs crossed behind him on the bed. Gently at first, I begin massaging circles on his back, starting at his shoulders. He groans appreciatively and doesn't stop me as I try to get the kinks out.

What is going on inside that head of his? When we first met, and even last night, he was stronger. But tonight? Tonight, he's off.

"Take your shirt off," I instruct so I can better massage him.

Without question, he sits up on his knees and pulls off his T-shirt, revealing his sculpted, tattooed body. I refrain from licking my lips, saved from the embarrassment of my ogling as he lies facedown again. Straddling his firm ass, I reach over to the nightstand and pour some of my lotion onto my hands. Starting along the spine, I slide my palms upwards, pressing deep along the way.

"Damn," he mumbles, voice muffled by the pillow.

I continue to work him over, focusing on tight areas and places that make him moan. As I rub him, I take my time inspecting his tattoos that color his back. He has a tribal tattoo intricately done on one shoulder blade. I've learned exactly what it looks like now that I've been massaging him for a bit.

"Talk to me, Thad," I urge as I press my fingers into the back of his neck.

He's quiet for a moment before he turns his head to the side. "I have issues, O. My childhood was unconventional, and I think I'm missing something in my genetic makeup that keeps me from doing stupid shit. I want to stay on the straight and narrow, but I honestly don't know how. My mother has always enjoyed playing her head games. Up until two months ago, my life had been spiraling out of control and I was on a path of self-destruction. Xanax and Jack were my best friends. One day, I'd had enough and checked into a rehab facility. The day we met was my first day back," he confides.

Stopping my massage, I congratulate him. "Thad, that's amazing though. You're two months sober. I'm so proud of you."

When he tenses beneath me, I suddenly realize he isn't finished.

"Tonight, I slipped up, O. Given the opportunity to drink, I took it. I downed an entire glass of liquor. I'm ruined. I'll never be able to fix the way I am." He sounds so melancholy and full of self-loathing. It breaks my heart for him.

Gently slapping his back, I clear my throat. "You're not ruined. Now roll over. I'll do your chest." Rising to my knees, I watch him flip to his back underneath me.

His sad eyes meet mine while I massage the contours of his chest. He closes his eyes about the same time that I feel his erection between us. I try to focus on the muscles that need to be kneaded and not grind myself against his dick. My hands slip over his hard pectorals to his collarbone. Then I bring them up the sides of his neck to thumb the prickly edges of his jaw. All of a sudden, his eyes fly open and his hands grip my wrists, startling me.

Now that I'm snared in his grasp, I stare down at him and inspect him closely. He's beautiful in every sense of the word. It's a challenge not to seize his lips with my own, but I promised him and myself friendship. Too bad his cock didn't get the message, because it is hardened to full mast between my legs now and it takes every ounce of self-control I possess not to ride it.

"You're not ruined, Thad," I remind him again. My heart sinks when he closes his eyes—I can see that he doesn't believe me.

He still has a death grip on my wrists. It's as if he thinks that, if he lets go, I'll bail on him too. I fucking hate his family for not being here when he needs them most.

"You make mistakes, just like I do. We're not perfect but that's okay. I could use a friend like you and I think you could use a friend like me as well," I tell him.

His eyes fly open and green orbs glare back at me. The intense stare he's giving me should scare me, but it turns me on instead. In a move that surprises me, he rolls us over until I'm underneath him, my wrists still in his grasp.

"I fucking hate that word, O," he growls and brings his nose to mine. I can smell the liquor on his breath, and I briefly wonder if I would be able to taste it on his tongue. "Admit you hate it too."

I do hate that word.

I'm suddenly hyperaware of all of my senses. His scent, the lingering smell of liquor mixed with soap, floods my nostrils and does things to my insides. My panties are growing wetter by the second as his cock nestles perfectly against my sweet spot through our clothes.

"I don't want to be your friend, O."

My clamp my eyes shut at his words. After the way he murmured that last sentence, I let go of any shred of sanity. Then he finally releases my hands and threads them in my hair. I can feel his hot breath against my lips, and I whimper with need for his touch.

He's giving me an out. Do I give in or break the rules I've set for myself? I slide my hands over his shoulders and link my fingers together to bring his head the last little bit to my lips.

"I don't want to be your friend either," I breathe.

And once again, the line has been crossed.

Chapter THIRTEEN

Thad

When my lips meet hers, the electric buzz that always flows when I am around Opal sparks to life. In an instant, our mouths are open and devouring one another. Right away, I notice she tastes like toothpaste and *her*—so fucking delicious. With a moan, she slides her hands into my hair and with each desperate kiss she tugs at my thick locks. My dick presses against her pussy, and this time, she digs her heels into my ass to better grind herself into me.

"I need to be inside you. Now," I murmur against her lips and then suck on her bottom one.

I find the edge of her nightshirt and slide my hand under the material until I locate her bare breast. Then I tease her nipple between my thumb and finger until it's nice and aroused. Moving my lips away from hers, I skim down her body and push her shirt up over her tits so I can view them properly. Leaning down, I take one into my mouth and suck reverently. Her mounds are the perfect size and shape—I could spend hours worshipping them. As I nibble at the flesh around her nipple, she nearly lifts off the bed as she whimpers my name.

"You like it when I bite you, O?" I question, slightly amused. For a good girl, she sure seems naughty.

Instead of answering me, she arches her back, which thrusts her tits in my face. I dip down again and tease her skin with my teeth. When she slips her hand down into her pajama bottoms, I groan because she's so fucking turned on. I nip her flesh once more, this time harder. Her fingers are rapidly going to town between her legs. Another nibble, this time on her other breast, causes her to convulse with her climax beneath me.

"Thad," she pants and softly cups my face with her free hand. "Take me."

Within seconds, I'm off the bed, yanking my jeans and boxers down. After pulling a condom from my wallet, I slide it on my throbbing cock, which is dying to be inside her. I wait impatiently as she pulls off her shirt but still has her bottoms on.

"These have to fucking go," I inform her as I grab the top and jerk them down her legs, tossing them to the floor.

As I climb on top of her, I behold the sight before me. She looks like a swirl of dark chocolate in a sea of vanilla that is her cream-colored comforter. When she spreads her legs for me, my cock rises impossibly higher. As much as I want to plunge it into her sweet pussy, I have the need to taste her first.

Her eyes widen when she sees what I'm about to do. "Thad, you don't have to. Nobody's ever—"

But before she can finish her sentence, I'm between her legs and spreading her pussy open with my thumbs. When I drag my tongue up her clit, which smells of lavender and tastes so fucking sweet, she attempts to scramble away from me.

"O, baby, you're going to love this," I promise and clutch her hips, dragging her back to my mouth.

This time, I attack her sweet nub with my tongue in a series of swirls and flicks that have her moaning in pleasure. I can tell she's getting close to climaxing again, so I slip a finger inside her while I give her clit a good suck.

She's overcome with trembles as another orgasm courses through her. Her tight pussy clenches around my finger as she rides it out, and I pull away to look up at her. Both of her hands are fondling her breasts and her head is tossed back. *This girl—damn!* She looks so fucking hot in the throes of passion. With a horny groan, I sit up on my knees and prepare to bang the shit out of this sexy-ass woman. Since her juices are still running out of her body, I wet the tip of my cock with her arousal and slowly push myself into her. Her heat instantly devours my dick and I want to come badly by the way her cunt constricts the hell out of me.

I ease myself down so that my chest presses against hers and then take her mouth once again with mine. Thrusting slowly into her, I enjoy being with her like this—her wanting me and being unrushed. Her pussy hugs my cock and we fuck like one well-oiled machine. I slide a hand under her head and pull her even closer to me. Not only have I wanted this woman like this for days, but I need to be with her. I was about to lose my mind after I stupidly downed that glass of alcohol. But the moment I touched Opal in the hallway, my worries and fears melted away.

"God, this feels—" she cries out but is cut off by my kisses.

I devour her, tasting every inch of her mouth and lips. Her hands find their way back up into my hair and she grips tight. I know I'm close to coming soon, and the moment I feel her come undone beneath me, I lose my load.

"Shit, O. You're a goddamned dream," I praise against her lips. After several more seconds of pumping into her, I roll us to our side so I don't smash her and pull her close to me.

"I can't believe you kissed me. You know, after," she confesses, wide-eyed. The innocent look on her face causes a chuckle to rumble in my chest.

"You taste sweet like honey. I wanted you to taste yourself. Did you not like it?" I inquire, quirking up an eyebrow.

A devilish grin turns the corners of her mouth up. "It was surprisingly hot," she admits.

"I'm glad you approve. I can't wait to show you a few more tricks, pretty girl."

She smiles broadly at me and bats her eyelashes, seemingly embarrassed by my words. I'm not sure if it's the prospect of doing naughty things or the fact I called her "pretty girl."

Testing my theory, I stroke her cheek and look into her eyes. "You're beautiful, O—like, drop-dead gorgeous. The moment I laid eyes on you, I knew you were special. Your body may sparkle with your glittery lotion shit, which I hope to God isn't what you massaged me with." I pause as she giggles. "But your heart fucking shines. I may not have known you for very long, but I do know that you wear your heart on your sleeve for all to see. You're kind, loyal, and caring. I'm lucky as fuck to have you in my arms right now."

Her grin falls to a frown as she strokes my back. "Thad, we're lucky. Not just you. You have shown me more affection and attention than any other man I've been with. It feels nice—to be treasured for once in my life."

We sit quietly for some time, staring at each other in comfortable silence. Finally, I voice what's worried me this entire time.

"What if I just royally fucked myself, O?" I squeeze my eyes shut in frustration.

She places a slender hand on my cheek and strokes it with her thumb. "Why do you think you fucked yourself? Because of the drink?"

I nod my head shamefully before opening my eyes back up to her compassionate, brown ones. "I can't go back to the person I was. There's no way. No fucking way. I want to do right. I have something good going on with my boss, Griff, and I have something great going on with you. I can't fuck it up, O."

"Shh, Thad. You're not going to fuck it up. I'll help you. We'll get through it together. I promise," she assures me and presses her lips to mine.

This woman has crawled into my heart and camped out. I hope to God she's as serious about me as I am about her.

I smile before deepening our kiss. "Let's do this."

The horror of last night's relapse was replaced by the perfection that is Opal. The moment this woman opened her apartment door last night, I felt the stress of the night lift. She has a way of dragging my dark thoughts to her light. I crave that light. We spent the entire night learning each other's bodies and talking about our childhoods. She, too, has a mother who bleeds icicles.

"Sir, what do you think about the paint color in the front room? I think it looks pretty badass." Manuel whistles as he comes into kitchen where I'm sanding the cabinets.

I could have hired this part out, but I love doing detailed woodwork when I can. Standing, I dust off my jeans and walk into the room to have a look. Things are quickly coming together, but when I see the color of the living room, I frown. What was supposed to be taupe looks purple.

"Shit, dude," I groan and rest my hands on my hips.

He looks around at his crew with confusion written all over his face. "You don't like it?"

I don't just not like it; I fucking hate it. "No, and it's my fault, Manuel. I need to rethink the color scheme. Have them just prime everything white for now until I can decide what we should do. How's it coming with the tile in the bathrooms?"

We spend the next few minutes going over the plans until the smell of Mexican takeout fills the space.

"Shit! Manuel, I have to jet. I almost forgot about my appointment. I'll see you guys later." I slap him on the shoulder and hurry out of the townhouse to Dad's Harley.

Minutes later, I'm cruising through traffic, heading toward my destination. When I find a spot in the garage, I'm nearly knocked over by some dickhead in a suit.

"Watch where you're going, asshole," I snap as he storms past me.

He grumbles a, "Fuck you," but I ignore him and step onto the elevator. The ride to the third floor is short. When I step into the lobby of the office area, a nice, older woman with her hair in a bun greets me.

"Are you Mr. Sutton?" she chirps.

I smile at her and nod.

"Nice to have you. Dr. Sweeney is just finishing up with someone and then he'll see you. Just complete this paperwork while you wait," she instructs. Her phone rings and she launches into a lengthy conversation, so I sit down to fill out the documents.

"Thank you, Dr. Sweeney," a female voice sniffles as the woman closes the office door behind her. She's a pretty one, probably one of Trent's types—long, blond hair, dressed to the nines in a suit, and mile-long legs. One would say she is beautiful—I'd say she's a sad woman harboring things that are ripping out her heart.

I watch her walk to the elevator, and with shaky hands, she presses the down button. Her purse slips from her clutches, slamming to the floor, sending contents flying across the marble. The receptionist gasps, but she is tied up on the phone, so I set the clipboard down and stride over to help the woman, who is now crying as she scrambles to scoop up her belongings.

I kneel down beside her and touch her shoulder. "Calm down. Let me help you."

She nods as tears stream down her face. I retrieve all of her things that have scattered all over the lobby floor and bring them to her so she can put them back in her purse. My hand hesitates when I go to give her back a bottle of antidepressants. She eyes me with interest, noting my hesitation, but doesn't say anything. Then I quickly hand them over to her and throw her one of my winning lopsided grins.

"Everything's going to be okay, ma'am," I assure her as we both stand.

In a movement that surprises me, she hugs me. "The name's Andi. And it's going to be okay for you too." She smiles at me knowingly.

"Thad. And I sure hope you're right," I reply as she releases me.

I flinch when she squeals and take a step away from the woman because she's quite possibly crazy.

"Thad? As in Thad In My Pants?" she questions with a huge grin.

It takes a moment for her words to register before I smile back at her. "You know O?"

"Oh my God!" She bounces up and down in her high heels. Yep, definitely on the nutty side. "You have a nickname for her. That's, like, the cutest thing ever! And you're so hot! No wonder she gets all flustered when she talks about you."

I chuckle at the thought of Opal being so affected by me. "I really like her, Andi," I confess, the corners of my mouth still upturned in a smile.

She launches at me again and knocks the breath out of me with one of her surprisingly strong hugs for such a slight woman. "I know! And this is great news. She's been pining after your oblivious brother for way too long. My girl deserves someone who sees her for the amazing person she is!"

As I hear the elevator doors open, I look over Andi's head and find the asshole from the parking garage.

"Are you quite done hugging my wife, motherfucker?" he growls at me, squaring his shoulders.

Andi jerks herself away from me and twirls around to face him. "Jackson Compton! For crying out loud! This is Trent's brother, Thad, you big caveman!" she snaps at him.

He's still glaring at me, so I cross my arms across my chest and smirk at him. "Someone had to comfort her since you left your own wife crying in the lobby while you were acting like a whiny-ass bitch."

My taunt successfully pushes its intended button, because he struggles to get to me. Poor Andi now has him in a bear hug, preventing him from kicking my ass.

"You must be Thaddeus Sutton," a deep voice calls to me from across the lobby.

I see an older gentleman leaning against the doorframe, looking none too pleased. Jackson flips me off once more before hauling Andi into the elevator with him. Fucking asshole.

"One in the flesh," I tell him cockily. God, I am in such a weird fucking mood now.

He glances over at me, frustration etching his features, and motions for me to follow him into his office. Once we're inside, I take a seat on the black leather sofa in front of his desk. The sofa looks new and is the epitome of the cliché couch you would find in a shrink's office.

"Did you have fun provoking him?" he asks, peering down over his glasses.

I huff and shrug my shoulders. "He was being a fucking asshole."

Looking down at his notebook, he writes something on his pad. Instantly, my guard is up.

"So, Thaddeus, it says here on your paperwork that you just completed rehab?"

I nod my head and lean back, crossing my arms over my chest. Now that I have Opal, I really feel like this visit is unnecessary. A few days ago, yes, I needed it. Now, not really.

"I see," he says and scribbles another note. Looking back up at me, he cuts right to the chase. "Have you had the desire since rehab to use drugs or drink alcohol?"

My eyes dart to his and my stomach clenches guiltily. "Uh, no," I lie.

He stares at me a few moments before he shakes his head. "I've been doing this far too long for you to lie to me and get away with it. Considering you even attempted lets me know that you have in fact thought about using. Now don't even try to avoid the inevitable. Let's be honest here. What we talk about stays here, Thaddeus. Have you used since you've left rehab?"

I think about my mother's deliberately setting me up and I'm suddenly and angrily grinding my teeth together. "I had a drink last night."

He looks back down to his clipboard and scribbles something again. It sets something off inside of me and I'm flooded with so many emotions: anger, confusion, sadness.

"What triggered you to take this drink you speak of?" he questions, his eyes off the clipboard and back on me.

I fidget in my chair as I debate telling him about my mother or not. Opal's face fills my thoughts and I realize I need to tell him if I want to get better. For her.

"My mother asked me to take her drink to the sink. We'd discussed some things that fucking pissed me off, and instead of pouring out the glass, I downed it," I reveal shamefully, myy eyes now inspecting the flooring in his office. The old hardwood could really use a refinishing.

"Do you think she set you up?" he asks, calmly. Everything about him is so cool and collected. It pisses me off.

"What do you think?" I snarl.

His eyes narrow briefly before he jots down another note. It drives me crazy when he does that.

"I think that you must believe she did in order to have gotten so angry. How is your relationship with your mother? What about the rest of your family?"

I sit up abruptly and dig my elbows into my knees while I thread my fingers through my hair. My mind is assaulted with angry thoughts toward my family, especially my mother. I also mourn for the child who grew up without the motherly love that is normal in most families. Bitterness also creeps into my veins over the fact that, because of her, I've become this mental head case.

"She's a callous bitch who thinks favoring one child over the other is normal. I've never met anyone in my life as cool and uncaring as she is. My father just does as he's told and has never had my back. My brother thinks I'm a loser and hates that I tarnish the family name," I huff out and sit back.

My blood is beginning to boil—just like it always does when I get fired up over the way they treat me. Usually, when I start to feel like this, I want to drink. Now, I start to bounce my foot up and down in an effort to dispel some of the pent-up energy pumping through me. I'm furious that I'm going through a spell of what normally sends me on one of my paths of destruction. Fuck my mother and her control over my mind.

Think of Opal.

Mentally picturing her tall, slender figure and gorgeous smile, I instantly feel myself relax.

I look up to see Dr. Sweeney writing. Again. Not being able to refrain from doing so, I roll my eyes at him. But he flicks he gaze up to mine when he asks his next question.

"What just happened there, Thaddeus?"

Confused, I shrug my shoulders.

"You went from being extremely angry to calm and collected. Something passed through your mind, and I'd like to know what that was," he responds.

"I thought of her. Opal. She's like the calm right now in the stormy sea that is my life. For once, I have something that helps me take my mind from all this shit."

He writes another note before his next question. "And how long have you known this woman?"

"A few days," I grumble, knowing that this will somehow be held against me by the frown now forming on his face.

"Hmmm," he murmurs before continuing. "Do you think it is fairly soon to have her already playing such a critical part in your life, Thaddeus? Like she might be your crutch? You've barely known her. You think it's healthy for someone in your emotional state to rely on another person to keep you calm?"

"Fuck this," I growl and stand quickly. But I pause when he raises his hand to stop me.

"Listen. I'm not trying to make you feel threatened. The truth is, I'm trying to help you. From your actions and your medical history, I think it is safe to say you're suffering from anxiety and depression. I'd even go as far as to guess you have manic episodes, which leads you to do impulsive things. I want you to start taking this mood stabilizer," he instructs and hands me a prescription. "It should help you to keep yourself on a more even playing field. And even though this woman keeps you from wanting to use, I think you need to be aware of the time you spend with her. I don't want you holing yourself inside with her, closing yourself off from the triggers of the real world. You can't avoid them. You must confront them. Take one of my cards. If you feel like using or the stress is too much, call my cell. I'll talk with you."

I accept the card and the prescription. Turning to leave, I'm stopped by his words again.

"Not so fast. I have homework for you."

Spinning around, I look at him quizzically. What sort of shrink gives homework? He's grinning at me because he obviously enjoys this shit.

"Thaddeus, I have a challenge for you. I want you start small—like with your brother—to begin to mend these broken relationships. It will be hard. That's why it's called a challenge. But I want you to really step out of your comfort zone. You're going to need to spend time with him and decide on things you can do together in a level playing field. When I see you next week, I want you to report back what happens during these visits. We'll eventually move on to your father and then your mother. If you feel like you're about to lose it, call me."

I close my eyes as I shove the prescription and his card into my pocket. Why in the fuck does he think I will do this shit?

You'll do it because of her.

Opal's face crosses my mind, reminding me that I need to man the fuck up and get myself well if I want to have a real chance of being with her.

"Okay. I'll try," I promise and mean it.

102

Chapter
FOURTEEN

Opal

From my position at my desk, I watch Jackson haul Andi into his office and slam the door behind him. He is beyond pissed. Poor Andi seems so sad. They are breaking my heart these days because I feel like there's a wedge in their relationship. I'm dragged from my thoughts when my phone rings. I grin stupidly when I see that Thad In My Pants is calling.

"I'm taking you out tonight, beautiful," he informs me by way of greeting.

I let out an amused giggle. "Oh, is that so?"

"O, that's so," he laughs. The rumble of his laughter niggles straight to my core.

I can't wait to see him again. He's awoken a sexual side I never knew I had before. Plus, I feel the need to protect him—from not only himself, but also his family.

Before I can say anything else, I hear the telltale banging of Jackson's credenza against the wall and bite back a grin.

"Pick me up at six," I instruct and hang up since Bray is striding over to my desk on a clear mission.

"What's up, Bray?" I ask while I add some papers to a file for Andi.

"Olive wants to have a get-together tomorrow night. She has an important announcement she wants to make and wants everyone there. Come over after work and we'll have dinner and drinks. Oh, and Abby told me this morning that she misses her Aunt Opie. So you better be there." He winks before he walks back into his office.

I'm still left reeling about what it is that Olive needs to tell us when a very flushed but smiling Andi slips out of Jackson's office. I cock an eyebrow up at her, letting her know I caught her in the act.

"Have fun in there banging shit around?" I laugh. "Or were you the one getting the shit banged out of you?"

"Opal!" Andi shrieks in embarrassment and practically runs to her office.

I'm still giggling when Jackson opens his office door and throws a smug grin my way before sauntering over to Jordan's door.

My phone rings on my desk and I chuckle when I see that it's Andi. "Miss me, hooch?" I tease in greeting.

"I can't believe you heard us!" Andi hisses into my ear.

"Andi, I always hear you guys, but it's been a while. I'm happy Stella got her groove back," I joke.

"Ugh! Anyway, guess who I ran into at Dr. Sweeney's?" she asks, her tone switching from embarrassed to one of excitement.

"Who?" I ask distractedly as I reply to an e-mail from the lady in human resources.

"Thad In My Pants!" she squeals so loudly I have to pull the phone from my ear.

Just hearing his name brings a huge smile to my face.

Thad.

"He's sexy as sin, huh?" I already know the answer though.

"Girl, he's sexy enough for Jackson to be jealous as hell and drag me back to the office for a quick claiming fuck!" she snorts.

We giggle like two school girls. But when we calm down, she turns serious.

"You know, Opal, people don't go to Dr. Sweeney unless they're fucked up like Jackson and me."

I frown as I consider her point. "I think everyone's a little fucked up to some degree," I affirm, "including myself."

"Well, I like him. I like him a hell of a lot more than I like Trent for you. Trent's a good guy, but this guy is a hunk. He looks dangerous, but he's sweet. I spilled my purse and he helped pick it all up for me—even telling me everything was going to be okay. I liked him instantly. I'm Team Thad In My Pants," she laughs. "Now get your ass in here and let's do some work," she commands in mock authority.

I roll my eyes at her tone and hang up. After snatching up the file I am working on, I waltz into the office of my best friend, where I know we'll spend more time giggling over men than actually working. *God, I love my job.*

A date with Thad.

What the fuck do I wear on a date with Thad? I've tried on at least fifteen dresses. When I went out with Trent, he always made sure to tell me how to dress.

Not Thad. No, that simply isn't his style.

Standing in nothing but my red lace bra and matching panties, I scan the closet once more for something to wear. I sigh in frustration when I hear the doorbell ring.

"Shit!" I curse and yank my white silk robe off the hook of my closet door. Hurrying to the out of my room, I slide the robe on along the way and tie it at the waist before opening the door. When I sling it open and see Thad standing there, my pissed-off attitude melts away. He's so freaking hot wearing in a pair of holey jeans and a black, tight Pink Floyd T-shirt. And I realize I've obsessed for nothing. He's dressed comfortably all the way down to his worn-out, black Doc Martens.

When my gaze meets his, I find his green eyes glowing with heat. Then I remember I'm wearing a little robe that barely covers my bottom and a smile tugs at my lips.

Before either of us can speak, he stalks into the apartment until he's pressed against my chest. I breathe in his delicious, soapy Thad scent and whimper when his hand slides around to cup my ass through the thin material. His other hand circles behind my neck and pulls me close to his lips.

"You're quite possibly the sexiest thing I've ever seen," he growls against my mouth.

Moisture builds between my legs as I slip my hands around to his muscular back and gently scratch him. My breath catches when he softly kisses my bottom lip. The tenderness is a contrast to the way he grips my ass—firmly and possessively.

He pulls his lips away and rests his forehead on mine, pinning me with his stare. Nobody has ever looked at me the way this man looks at me. I could get drunk off his gaze.

"If you don't get dressed now, I'm going to be tempted to fuck you right here up against this wall," he threatens as he pushes me up against it, his thick erection pressed into my belly.

He dips his lips down to my neck and sucks me lightly, causing me to gasp. The hand he has on my ass glides to my front and pulls one of the strings to my robe. When it opens up, it reveals my breasts, which are practically spilling out of my red lace bra.

"You have the hottest fucking body on the planet," he groans as he trails kisses down to the swell of my breasts. His compliments flow right into my heart, and I smile.

Both of his hands skim over to my hips and drag my panties down my thighs as he kisses my flesh along the way. The man is a tattooed beauty knelt down in front of me and I need more of him. As if answering my wish, he urges my legs apart and slips a finger between them before pushing it inside me, my smile falls. *My God, he feels so damn good.*

"You're so wet for me," he observes in a voice that's raspy, thick with desire.

He pushes his finger deep into me and I moan loudly as I grab two handfuls of his hair. His finger drags my wetness in and out of me in such a way that I want more than just his finger.

"Thad, I need you," I beg.

Instead of answering, he tongues between the lips of my pussy and I gasp. Then he begins lapping me up like I'm a delicious melting ice cream cone. His eagerness to taste me has me getting wetter and wetter for him.

106

"That's it, baby. Give it to me. I want to lick up every drop," he instructs huskily.

His finger continues to fuck me, drawing out more and more of my juices as he licks me. But it isn't enough; I need more of him. As if understanding my need, he grabs the ankle of one of my legs and hoists my foot onto his shoulder, opening me up more to him.

He pulls his finger out and I whimper at the loss, but that whimper quickly becomes a moan as he replaces it with his tongue. His tongue is long and strong as it pushes inside me, creating a slippery, fucking amazing sensation. I'm not even embarrassed when I realize I'm shoving his head closer to me, needing him more.

I've never been so wet in my life. He's killing me with the way he keeps fucking me with his tongue as his thumb starts massaging my clit. My leg begins shaking as I'm hit with a whole-body-encompassing orgasm.

"Holy shit!" I cry out and nearly collapse from the intensity. The things this man can do with his tongue should be illegal. *But I'd gladly break the rules for more.*

He urges my foot off his shoulder and onto the floor before he stands. When he brings his lips to mine, I'm strangely turned on as I see his face glistening with my arousal. Then he kisses me softly.

"You taste amazing, O. Your flavor is intoxicating—fucking delicious. I've never wanted to consume every drop from any woman like the way I want to do with you. You're addicting, like my own fucking drug."

I want this man. More than any man I've ever wanted in my entire life. Even Trent—the man I relentlessly threw myself at for four years of my life. With Thad, it all comes easily, naturally. I enjoy the flutter in my heart as my hand makes it down his hard cock, which is pressed between us. I want to touch him, taste him, worship him like he does me.

"Your turn, hot stuff," I instruct saucily.

The shocked but excited look he gives me is all the confidence I need as I slide down his body to properly service him as well.

Chapter FIFTEEN

Thad

She tastes like fucking honey—sweet and delicious. When she kneels in front of me, her robe still hanging open, and begins unfastening my jeans, I nearly come from the sight of her. She's perfect. Chocolate skin, smooth as silk. Long, dark hair hanging perfectly down her shoulders. A look of determination is painted on her face as she pulls my thick cock from my boxers.

She hesitantly strokes my length as she runs her tongue from the base up to the tip. I can tell that, just like everything else with her, she's inexperienced. I'm not going to lie though—it makes me fucking happy to get to experience things she's never done before with her. My thoughts disappear as her supple lips suck my dick.

"O, fuck!" I gasp as my hands slip into her hair.

She begins bobbing her head up and down, tentatively seeing how deep she can take me into her mouth. I can't think about anything except the way her tongue is rubbing against my flesh and the scrape of her teeth against my shaft every so often. It feels so goddamn good that I know I am on the brink of coming.

"Pretty girl, I'm going to come," I warn with a hiss as I feel myself getting closer.

It only seems to encourage her, and she picks up her pace, trying her damnedest to suck the come right out of me. Seconds later, I explode into her mouth with a groan. She chokes for a moment from the surprise of my load but quickly swallows it down before pulling off my cock to look up at me.

Her eyes are filled with pride—and hope.

"You're really good at that," I chuckle.

She laughs as she climbs back to her feet after tucking me back into my pants. I have to tear my gaze from her tits, which are spilling out of her bra, so that we can focus on getting out of here for our date.

"As much as I want to toss you over my shoulder and spend the rest of the night doing naughty things to you, I promised you a date." I grin at her. "Now, go get dressed, sexy." I swat her ass for effect.

She giggles, pushing away from me to head to her room. My eyes follow her curvaceous bottom as she sashays out of the room, purposefully swinging her hips along the way.

"You'll pay for that later," I threaten.

More laughter comes from her room as I hear her banging drawers as she searches for clothes. While she dresses, I pull my phone from my pocket and try to grow the balls to message my brother. Dr. Sweeney said to start small, but the beef between Trent and me is anything but small—and the fact that he's slept with Opal only adds to our problems. I groan in annoyance but bite the bullet and text him.

Me: Want to meet for lunch tomorrow? To talk?

My heart is racing nervously. I want nothing more than to make my life right, and if it means attempting to have a relationship with my brother, then so be it. I'll try anything at this point.

Seconds later, he sends a response that has me cursing under my breath.

Trent: Talk about what? I have meetings all day.

I clench my jaws together and decide that I'm not going to respond. If he doesn't realize there's a problem between us, then fuck him. I'm just tucking my phone into my pocket when it chimes again.

Trent: I rearranged my schedule. Want to meet at Zoe's Pizzeria around noon?

A grin involuntarily spreads across my face. I haven't been to Zoe's since I was ten—right before Trent and I began to drift apart. Our parents used to take us there to expel some of our energy on video games. Zoe's sells alcohol, so Mom and Dad would essentially have a date night while my brother and I would keep ourselves entertained for a couple of hours.

"I'm beating your ass!" I laugh as I pound on the buttons of the machine. I never beat Trent, but today, I'm killing him.

"You can't say ass, Thad. Mom will get mad," he says through clenched teeth while he tries desperately to catch up to my score on the game.

Trent has always been the one to keep an eye on me when Mom isn't standing over my shoulder. He's kept me in line and the older I get, the more I am beginning to resent it.

"Ass! Ass! Ass! Prepare to be dominated!" I taunt, trying to throw him off his game.

It works, because he punches me in the arm. He's strong for twelve, so I let go of the joystick to rub my arm for a second. I can see that he's catching up, so I hurry back to pounding the button with my hand.

Moments later, the music starts playing, indicating that I won. "Yeah!" I shout and fist-pump the air. Trent glares at me, but when I start dancing like MC Hammer and telling him he "can't touch this," he starts laughing.

"Thad, you're such a dork! You cheated!" he exclaims, trying to force his smile away. But now I've moved on to doing the lawnmower man dance and he can't help but be entertained by me.

"I didn't cheat and you know it. Don't be a sore loser!" I tell him, out of breath. I'm winded from my little show.

"Time to go, boys," Mom's voice calls out to us.

I frown as I realize the fun is over. When I look up at Trent, he's grinning at me.

"Good job, little brother. I taught you everything you know," he laughs with a wink before walking away toward Mom and Dad.

My heart swells with pride. My brother thinks I did a good job.

Nothing can get rid of the smile that's plastered on my face as I leave. Trent finally thinks I did a good job.

Me: See you then, bro. Prepare to be dominated.

"What's so funny?" Opal asks, coming out of the bedroom.

My smile falls when I see her. She's always so fucking beautiful—even when she isn't trying.

"Uh, nothing," I mutter as she comes into full view. Her legs look a mile long in a dark pair of skinny jeans. I laugh at the T-shirt shirt she's wearing. "Justin Timberlake?" I question, cocking up an eyebrow.

Huffing, she puts her hands on her hips. "What's wrong with JT?" she demands and then proceeds to do a cute little dance. "I'm bringing sexy back."

Honestly, there isn't a fucking thing wrong. The shirt is tight and she looks hot as hell wiggling her tits at me as she 'brings sexy back.'

"Come on," I growl, grabbing her hand and pulling her to the door. "We'll never agree on music and I'm about two seconds from ripping that shirt from your body, so we better leave. *Now.*"

She gasps. "What is your obsession with ripping clothes off my body?"

I throw her a smug grin, "With a body like that, clothes are fucking criminal. I'm doing this world a service, sugar. Eventually, you won't have any left—and you won't hear me crying over that notion."

We've been walking hand in hand for a good twenty minutes, passing bars and restaurants. Not once does she ask where we're going. Instead, she just smiles as she takes in the scenes of it all. It doesn't go unnoticed by me that every man we pass eyes up my girl. She's a fucking showstopper and doesn't even realize it.

"We're here," I tell her as I pull her toward the door of the old Mexican restaurant. It's one of my favorite places to go, not only for the amazing food but for the live bands they always have playing.

"Smells amazing, Thad," she tells me appreciatively as I guide her inside and to a booth near the stage.

The restaurant isn't too busy, so we easily find a place. I hope she's not turned off that I took her to a hole-in-the-wall restaurant—but they truly do have great food. She scoots into the booth and I sit down beside her, putting my arm around her. Her eyes cut to mine and she smiles before she opens the menu.

The band starts playing, so when the server comes by, we have to shout our order. I pull Opal closer to me so I can have access to her ear since it's so loud.

"Having fun?" I question and nip her lobe with my teeth.

Her hand finds my thigh and squeezes. Turning to me, she raises an eyebrow and says, "I'll have more fun later when we're alone."

My cock springs to life as it always does when I'm around her. I find her ear once more, dipping my tongue in briefly. "You're my calm, O. I don't even think about using around you. You keep me centered."

Suddenly, Dr. Sweeney's words flood my mind. *"Do you think it is fairly soon to have her already playing such a critical part in your life, Thaddeus? Like she might be your crutch? You've barely known her. You think it is healthy for someone in your emotional state to rely on another person to keep you calm?"*

"My therapist thinks I'm using you as a crutch," I admit with a grumble.

The caresses on my thigh stop and she turns to look at me again. "A crutch?" she asks, biting her bottom lip. I can see the wheels turning in her head.

"He also thinks I need to make amends with Trent and my parents, so, clearly, he's just a quack," I joke.

She doesn't laugh though. "I know that Dr. Sweeney helps Andi and Jackson, but that's just ridiculous. I'm sorry, but your family are assholes to you," she snips out.

I pull her closer and press my lips to hers. It's nice to have someone on my side for once.

Then she breaks our kiss and says, "Besides, if being with me keeps you from doing drugs or drinking, why is that a bad thing?"

"You have a point there, pretty girl. As long as I have you, I'll be just fine," I assure her.

The rest of dinner goes by without any other weird moments—the band is great, the food is awesome, and the company is the best. Before long, we're taking another walk, this time with Opal tucked under my arm. It feels right being with her. I am fucking invincible.

"Come on. I want to show you something," I tell her as I hail a cab.

After a steamy make-out session in the back of the cab, we finally pull up to our destination. Then I pay the cab driver and we make our way up to the townhouse I've been remodeling.

"What's this?" she questions, a hint of excitement in her voice. The anticipation within her words validates that bringing her here was a good idea.

"I'm remodeling this townhouse. It's what I do for a living. My crew has already been hard at work," I answer while I fumble with the keys in the dark. Finally, I manage to get the door opened and flip on the switch. Manuel and the guys have finished most of the living room and hallways. We're just waiting on my word on the paint color.

"Wow. It's a beautiful place," she gushes while she admires the work so far. "That color has to go though." Her nose is turned up as she points to the living room wall color.

I chuckle at her words because I thought the same damn thing. "Maybe you can help me out with that," I laugh as I snatch the paint book from the floor beside some paint cans and hand it to her.

Her eyes widen and she starts flipping very seriously through the book, looking back and forth between the space and the colors. "With those big windows allowing in all that light, you could get away with a bolder color than that taupe. A dark-khaki color would be perfect because then you could accent with just about any color scheme you want," she tells me animatedly. Her face is so fucking cute as she squats to pick up a tape measure.

I'm grinning at her as she flutters about the living room measuring windows and floor space. "Having fun?" I ask her for the second time tonight.

"Duh! You know I love this stuff," she beams.

She truly does. I've seen her magazines and notes. Her apartment is straight out of a magazine.

I finally ask what I've wondered all along. "If you love interior design so much, why are you working at the architectural firm?"

She frowns and shrugs her shoulders. "Because they took me in when I needed it most. And now, my degree will take me to the accounting department there. They've always been good to me—I'd hate to let them down."

Now it's my turn to furrow my brows. "O, by pleasing everyone else, you're letting *you* down. Why not go after what you want? What you *really* want—not just what you think you want?"

She bites her lips and shrugs off my questions, seeking refuge in the kitchen. "Wow, Thad! This kitchen is amazing!" she praises, sliding her palm across the granite. My chest swells with pride—the kitchen is my baby.

I stride over to her and hug her from behind. "I want your help, O. Your knowledge and eye for detail could really be useful. We could go shopping together and get the right appliances, paint, and whatever else you think would look good. I'd love to get your opinions to make this place badass and over-the-top luxurious. My career is kind of riding on if I can pull this off or not. Griff is counting on me. And I know you'd have a blast doing it. So what do you say? Want to be a part of this?"

She turns in my arms and wraps her arms around my middle. "I'd love to help you."

I kiss her forehead and pull away because I can feel her practically buzzing with excitement. She's already steaming ahead in designer mode.

"I love the comfortable feel this townhome has. So, I think with some sleek stainless-steel appliances in here, they'll complement the cherry wood cabinets. Modern yet warm. Thad, this is so exciting!"

I laugh and follow her as she bounces around, measuring things and writing down notes. A couple of times, she takes photos with her phone. After she's thoroughly inspected the entire space, she grabs my hand.

"Come on. Let's go back to my place and we can look stuff up on the computer."

I raise an eyebrow at her. "Are you sure you aren't just trying to lure me back to your apartment so I can take advantage of your sweet little body?"

She playfully swats at me. "Hmm… I'll let you wonder. It's always best to keep a little mystery in a relationship."

I watch her cute little ass wiggle right out the front door.

"Wow. I can't believe we just ordered all that stuff. Are you sure that was okay?" she asks, biting her bottom lip.

We spent the better part of two hours researching fixtures, paint techniques, and appliances. I agreed with all of her choices and placed the orders so my crew can install everything later this week.

"Of course it is. Stop worrying. This remodel is going to kick ass by the time we finish."

She smiles when I say *we*, and my heart swells with pride that I'm helping her be a part of something she truly enjoys.

"Thad, I had a lot of fun tonight. I haven't been on many dates, but this was by far my favorite one."

I grin and slide a hand over her thigh. "Babe, the night's not over. I have a lot more fun in store for you."

She giggles when I grab her hips and pull her into my lap. I groan when her sexy-ass long legs straddle me, and she doesn't hesitate to dive right in to kiss me. While she tastes me, I take the opportunity to slide my hands to her ass and squeeze it.

"God, this ass is so hot," I groan between kisses.

When my cock flares to life, she starts rocking against it. I wanted to take things slow with her, but now, all I can think about that is there are too many fucking layers of clothes between us.

"I need you naked, like, yesterday."

She nods and goes to climb off, but I stop her. Instead, I easily stand up with her and stride into the bedroom. Once we get to the bed, I set her down and we start shedding clothes like the world is ending. As soon as we're both naked, I locate a condom from my wallet and roll it on.

"What do you want, pretty girl?" I want her to know that I'll do anything for her. All she has to do is ask.

Her lips curl into a mischievous smile and she scoots onto the bed. With a curved finger, she motions for me to come to her. *Oh, I'll be coming all right.*

"I want you, Thad. Rough and raw. I want you to fuck me hard. Spank me, bite me, suck me. And then, when I can't take anymore, I want you to make love to me. Slow and sweet."

I blink in shock at her boldness, but my cock is rock hard.

A frown tugs at her lips. "Or just whatever you want to do. I thought we were talking about our fantasies and I didn't realize—"

I cut her off by pressing a thumb to her lips and then point a long finger at her. "You, pretty girl, can have whatever the fuck you want. If you want to be naughty, I'll give you fucking naughty."

She smiles broadly. Trust isn't something I give easily, and I can see that she's the same way. Together, though, we can do this.

"Bad little girls need to get on their knees," I growl.

Her lips form into a sexy little pout meant to tease me. My cock throbs accordingly. She got the reaction she wanted. With a satisfied laugh, she gets on her hands and knees, baring her sweet little ass.

"What's my crime? I always thought I was a good girl."

I climb onto the bed behind her and give her a soft swat on her bottom. "You thought wrong. I want you to stop trying to please everyone else and go after what you want. So, next time I ask what you want, just tell me. I'll do my damnedest to help you achieve that."

"Okay," she whimpers as she awaits my next move.

I slide my hand along her ass and dip a finger right into her hot pussy. "Do you like me here?" I ask as I finger-fuck her slow and deep.

"Yes," she moans out.

While my finger is inside her, I slap her bottom harder this time. "And did you like that or is it too much?"

"Yes, more."

I smile down at this beautiful woman who practically begging me to take her to new sexual heights. "Oh, I can give you more."

With the tip of my finger, I caress her G-spot deep within her. When she flinches, I know I have got it.

"Feel that, O?"

"Mmmhmm."

"That's mine," I murmur possessively and stroke it over and over until I know she's close to coming.

I withdraw my finger a bit and slap her ass hard again. And while I rub away the sting, I slide my finger back in, owning the pleasure button inside her. When an orgasm seizes her and she squirms away from the intensity of it, I dig my fingers into her hip and pull her back to me.

"Did you like that?"

"Yes," she breathes out in reply.

"Good, because I'm ready to give you more. Now crawl over to the headboard and hold on."

She yelps when I pull my finger out but obeys. I want in her tight little pussy, but first things first—to get a little crazy with my sex goddess.

"Do you have any rope?" I question as I step off the bed.

"Rope? No. I have some scarves though, hanging in the closet."

Perfect. I saunter into the closet and retrieve three. When I come back into the room, I really have to refrain from losing my load like a prepubescent schoolboy seeing a naked woman for the first time. She looks so fucking erotic as she grips the headboard, her hair hanging wildly down her back.

Gently, I take her hand and wrap one of the scarves around her wrist. Then I fasten it to one of the posts on the bed. She doesn't make a peep as I go around to the other side and secure her there too. With the last scarf, I loosely tie it around her eyes, blocking her vision.

When I climb back onto the bed behind her, I let my dick press against her ass.

"See how much I want you?" I groan.

Her response is a ragged gasp, but as I slide a hand around to her belly, a whimper escapes her. As I crouch down and place a soft kiss on the small of her back, my palms find their way to her hips. My thumbs rub circles on her ass cheeks as I alternate between kissing and sucking all over that sweet, curvy butt of hers.

"Spread your knees apart," I command hoarsely. There's so much I want to do to her body, but I have to get a handle on my throbbing cock first.

She complies and spreads herself as far as she can go. *Fuck me, this woman is hot.* Her pussy tightens around my finger as I push into her hot center to see if she's still wet for me. *Hell yeah, she is.* When I pull it back out, she cries out from the loss and pushes her ass toward me. She wants this just as bad as I do.

"That sweet little pussy of yours is begging to be pounded," I growl.

"Yes, please," she begs.

Instead of giving in right away, I tightly grip her hips again and trail kisses along the swell of her ass.

"Thad, you're such a tease," she whines and wriggles her butt at me.

I give her a spank hard enough for her to yelp and buck away from me. "Playtime's almost over, baby. I'm about fuck you into to-morrow. Every time you sit down at work, you're going to think of me stretching that tight pussy of yours."

And boy, do I spend the rest of the night making good on my promise.

Chapter
SIXTEEN

Opal

I wince as I ease myself into my desk chair. Thad left me quite sore but in a way that had me wanting more—and soon. Sex with Drake had always been traumatic and awful. And then sex with Trent was severely underwhelming. But sex with Thad? He is in a whole other league.

Sex with Thad is addicting.

"Dreaming about your lover boy?" a familiar voice giggles.

I glance up from where I was dreamily staring off into space to look my best friend in the eye. I'm still grinning like an idiot until I see her eyes—they're swollen from crying. My heart squeezes for her.

"Yes, as a matter of fact, I was. But what's up with you? Are you okay?" I ask softly. My eyes flit over to Jackson's office, but the door is closed. It's always closed when he's being pissy.

Andi plasters on a fake smile and nods. Tears are welling in her eyes, so I know that she is not okay.

"Liar. What's up? Are you and Jackson having a fight?"

Before she can answer, his door dramatically swings open and he storms over to her. Instead of shrinking away from his hostile attitude, she melts into his arms when he envelops her in a tight embrace.

"I'm sorry," he murmurs into her hair and kisses her as if I'm not sitting there, watching them. I feel slightly awkward about having to witness their exchange.

She cries into his chest as he leads her back into his office and closes the door behind them. I'm glad they're seeing Dr. Sweeney, even if he is a quack. They worry me these days, and I'll be glad when they sort out their problems so Andi can go back to being her happy, fun-loving self.

An e-mail pops up on my computer and I hold my breath once I realize that it's from Dr. Ellis.

Opal,
I've arranged for you to come into my clinic for DNA testing at your earliest convenience. I appreciate you doing this for me. If you come in this morning, maybe I could take you to lunch after?
Sincerely,
Martin

I release the breath I was holding. Yesterday, I agreed to do the testing, but now, I'm nervous. I've gone my entire life not knowing my father, and suddenly, I have someone claiming to be him. As much as I don't want to talk to my mother, I know I need to speak to her about Dr. Ellis. Quickly, I type out a reply to the man who says that he's my father and then dial my mother.

"Hello?" she answers in the clipped, annoyed tone I've been familiar with my entire life.

I swallow down my discomfort. She and I haven't spoken in ages. "Hi, Momma."

She's silent on the other line, which only adds to my irritation. Why can't she be a normal freaking mother?

"I'm graduating in two weeks," I begin hesitantly. I figure that it's best to talk about something lighter before I drop a bomb in her lap.

"And?"

I roll my eyes and struggle not to hang up on her ass. "*And*," I snip out, "I thought you would want to watch your youngest daughter walk across stage."

"New York is a long way. I'm not sure I can afford to fly out," she sighs. Her voice is softer this time, so I stupidly hope she's lost some of her frostiness.

"Momma, don't worry about it. I'll buy your ticket. And you can stay with me or Olive. Or, if you'd rather, I can put you up at a hotel. I'd really like for you to come. Plus, I know Olive wants to see you. Her husband and daughter are really special people—and they want to meet you," I rush out.

I'm met with silence again.

"Momma?"

"I heard you, child. I'll think about it. Now, is that all you called for?"

Anger replaces my hopefulness and I feel like throwing my phone at Jackson's door—which would really give him something to be pissed about.

"No. Actually, Momma, I wanted to speak to you about something else. Something important."

Her annoyed sigh is audible, and I take a deep, calming breath before speaking again.

"Who is my father?"

She curses under her breath, which surprises me. My highly religious mother never curses. "Opal, for crying out loud, what is all of this about? Like I told you before, your father left us long ago. End of story. Now, I'll speak to you another day. I really must go now."

I blurt out my next words before I can stop myself. "Is Martin Ellis my father?"

A rush of exhaled breath into the phone is her first reaction. "How do you know that name?" she hisses shakily into the phone.

My heart flutters into overdrive. I wasn't expecting her response to indicate that she knew him, but I can hear the surprise in her voice—she does, in fact, know him.

"He wants a paternity test done to see if I'm his daughter," I tell her softly.

"Opal Elaine Redding! This is absolute nonsense. You are not his daughter! Absolutely ridiculous," she bellows into the phone.

I won't back down now. She has answers and I intend to get them.

"I want to know my real father, Momma. If Dr. Ellis is my dad, then I want to have a relationship with him."

"Doctor," she whispers out wistfully.

"I'm going to take the test after we hang up."

I hear her sniffle and my heart clenches. She still cares for him—but in true Momma fashion, she steels her voice again.

"He is not your father, Opal. Please don't take the test."

"There's no stopping me. I'll let you know the results," I advise her firmly.

I nearly drop the phone when she explodes. "You take that test and you are dead to me! Do you hear that, Opal? *Dead. To. Me.*"

Chuckling darkly, I remind her, "I thought I already was."

A dial tone is her comeback, and I angrily slam my phone on my desk. Needing to take a breather, I gather my purse and stand from my desk. I'll just head over to Dr. Ellis's office early. I pick my phone up and shoot Andi, who still hasn't emerged from Jackson's office, a text. Storming over to the elevators, I'm nearly knocked on my ass when over six feet worth of familiar manliness slams into me.

"Opal?" Trent asks as he steadies me by holding my upper arms.

When my eyes meet his clear, blue ones, I want to throw up. While he's a good-looking guy—one I dreamed about for years—he just doesn't fuel that inner fire like Thad does. And after our awful sexual encounter, I know we're lacking in the chemistry department.

"I'm sorry, but I'm late," I stammer out and struggle away from his hold. Pushing past him, I hurry into the elevator and press the ground floor button.

"Opal, wait. I need to apologize about the other night—"

Thankfully, the elevator doors close mid-sentence and I'm granted a reprieve from his embarrassing apologies. During the entire ride down the fifty-seven floors, I try to calm my nerves. Between the upcoming DNA test, the conversation with my mother, and running into Trent, I'm completely rattled.

As the doors open, my phone chimes with a text from my purse. I fish it out and frown.

`Trent: Opal, I'm so sorry. I need to see you again.`

I sigh but know that a conversation between the two of us is inevitable. My sudden lack of interest in him, especially after we slept together, has to be confusing for him. I need to sever any ideas he might have of us ever being together again.

Me: Let's meet for lunch tomorrow. Pick me up at noon.

"We'll call you with the results in two business days, Miss Redding," the nurse tells me.

I thank her and walk back over to my chair to wait for Dr. Ellis. Before I sit down, I hear him call out to me.

"Opal, I'm so glad you made it."

When I turn to him, he's beaming happily at me. My heart flops as I look him over. Could this sweet man really be my father? I try desperately to find any similarities in our appearances. He's tall like I am, but that's not unusual for a man. His eyes are a lighter shade of brown than mine, as is his skin. I try not to frown as I realize I look too much like my mother to be able to see any similarities.

He picks up the file from the nurse's desk and briefly glances over it before setting it down. When he looks back up at me, his smile is impossibly bigger.

"Ready?" he asks as he strides over to where I'm standing.

Things will seem more comfortable once I know for sure if he's my father or not. Right now, the air between us feels awkward and unsure on my part, while he seems overly hopeful. For his sake, I hope the test reveals that we are a match.

"Sure. Where should we go?" I question nervously.

He seems like he's about to pull me in for a hug, so I take a step toward the door. For some reason, I don't want to get my hopes up about this man. As much as I would like to know my father, I can't force the one in front of me to be him simply because he's a cool guy. I need proof before I can open my heart up to him.

"There's an Italian restaurant on the corner. We can walk. They have the best manicotti in town. Would that be okay?" From the look in his eye, I could probably tell him that I want McDonald's and he'd agree.

"Perfect." What I fail to mention is that manicotti is my favorite. Is it a coincidence that he's suggesting my favorite food?

Opal, get it together. There's a huge chance that he's not your father.

I'm quiet the entire walk to the restaurant, only nodding in response to his nervous chatter about everything under the sun. After we've been seated and each ordered the famous manicotti, I finally speak again.

"What did you ever see in her, Dr. Ellis?" I question in disbelief. Honestly, I can't begin to understand how such a nice person could ever be remotely interested in a mean woman like my mother.

His smile falls and he regards me with a longing look as he remembers her. "Opal, first of all, please call me Martin. *At least for now.*"

I swallow down his insinuation that he might like for me to call him Dad one day.

He continues. "The Yolanda you know and the one I knew sound like two totally different people. She was feisty, I'll give you that. But she had a huge heart. She loved Olive and protected her fiercely. I was impressed at what a wonderful mother she was to that little girl. That's why I'm surprised to hear the animosity in your voice toward her."

I tear off a piece of bread and chew it as I mull over his words. Wonderful mother? On what planet? After I swallow it down, I look back up into his warm, brown eyes.

"Martin, she's vile. The word wonderful and Momma don't even belong in the same sentence. Do you know that she hardly even speaks to Olive anymore? That she hasn't even seen her only grandchild, who happens to be four years old? She even seems bothered about coming to my graduation at CUNY in two weeks—even after I offered to pay her way *and* give her a place to stay. She's not so wonderful anymore."

He frowns at my words, and I feel guilty about having gone off on him about her.

"I'm sorry she's been horrible to you. She wasn't always that way. Had she allowed herself to love me, maybe things could have been different for you. In some ways, I feel responsible for that," he tells me sadly.

I feel bad for the man sitting in the booth across from me—the man pining for my bitch of a mother. If only he knew. And the guy's quick to take responsibility for her actions. Who is this man? Some kind of saint?

My father, the saint. Kind of has a ring to it.

Shit. He's probably not your father, Opal.

"It's not your fault," I say softly.

He forces a smile and visibly pushes away thoughts of my mother. I can see it written all over his face that he wants to remember her as the woman he loved all those years ago.

He clears his throat and smiles more broadly at me. "Tell me about this graduation you speak of."

I can't help the grin that tugs at my lips. This man, even though there's only a chance he could be my father, seems proud at my achievement.

"I'll be graduating with a degree in investments. It's just a bachelor's degree," I reply, my voice dropping on the last sentence. I was proud until the Ice Queen, Dr. Sutton, shot me down.

"*Just* a bachelor's degree? Opal, I'm delighted to hear that. You've worked hard in your studies. That's to be commended. Don't sell yourself short, kid."

Opal, he's probably not your father. Wipe that stupid grin off your face.

"Sorry. I was recently made to feel like that wasn't enough," I confide.

His face hardens and my heart nearly leaps from my chest. The look is one of utter protectiveness—a look only a father would have as he protects his child.

He is not your father…

"Well, that person is an asshole," he grumbles.

I can't help the giggles that burst from me at his statement. The curse word coming from the older man seems out of place but funny nonetheless. He rewards me with a crooked smile—a smile that warms me to my soul.

Please be my father.

"That person is a she. Total asshole. Actually more like total bitch," I agree.

With a chuckle, he tears the top of the paper from the straw and blows it over at me. I dodge it and it flies over the booth behind us.

"Hey!" I laugh.

His smile once again falls and his face reflects sadness. "Opal?"

"Yes?" I tear off another piece of bread and begin chewing.

"Elaine is my mother's name."

Swallowing down the bread, I try not to choke on not only my food, but his words as well. "That's my middle name," I whisper finally.

He winks at me. "I looked at your chart. I know."

I blink at him in disbelief. Coincidence?

Raising his glass of water to me, he grins at me. "Here's to hoping, kid."

Here's to hoping you're my dad.

With a smile, I raise my glass too.

Chapter SEVENTEEN

Thad

As I walk into Zoe's Pizzeria, I'm assaulted with delicious, garlicky aromas and fond memories. I'm feeling nostalgic as my eyes scan the small restaurant, bringing me visions of a happier time in my life. The tattered, vinyl, red-and-white-checkered tablecloths are the same as I remember. Several aging arcade relics sit tiredly along the wall, occasionally chiming familiar tunes.

"Take a seat wherever you like," a friendly hostess smiles, interrupting me from my reminiscing.

Realizing that I'm here before Trent, I find a table in the corner and sit down. Recent conversations with my brother haven't been enjoyable ones, so I'm slightly anxious about our meeting. While I wait for Trent, I pull out my phone and call Opal.

"How's your day going?" I ask once her voice greets me on the other end.

"Actually, pretty well. I just had lunch with the man who may or may not be my father," she says cryptically.

With one statement, I realize that we still know so little about each other.

"Sounds interesting, O. I think you and I should have story time later," I laugh.

She giggles on the other end and a dorky grin spreads across my face.

"Does this story time take place in bed?" she purrs.

I groan as I feel my cock thicken from just imagining her in bed. "Story time in bed will have to take place right after work."

"Rain check, Thad. I actually wanted to ask you something. Tonight, I'm supposed to be going over to my sister's for dinner. Would you like to come?"

"Of course, Opal. I'd love to meet your sister."

Her breath is heavy into the phone as she sighs her relief. Did she really think I'd say no? To hell with that—she's not getting rid of me that easily.

When the bell on the door of the restaurant sounds, my eyes lift and automatically meet those of my brother. "I'll pick you up after work at your house, O. Talk soon."

We hang up just as Trent saunters over to the booth and sits down across from me. Neither of us says anything for a brief moment as we eye up the other. He's Mr. Perfect, of course, with his styled, blond hair and impeccable suit, while I'm the lowly brother in my dirty work jeans and worn, gray Foo Fighters T-shirt.

"What's up, bro?" My voice is low, nervous almost.

He huffs out a breath of frustration and crosses his arms over his chest, looking me squarely in the eyes. "I don't know, little bro. You tell me. You're the one taking time out of my work day to 'talk.' So talk."

Fucking asshole.

My mind is flooded with images of seeing him with Opal the night she and I met. The night he made her feel like nothing by calling her a friend. Then, a couple of nights later, when he was passed out on his bed after fucking her—my woman—wearing nothing but a used condom. Rage bubbles to the surface and I angrily slam my fist down onto the table.

"Fuck you, Trent," I seethe between gritted teeth.

His face softens as he raises his hands in mock surrender. "Thad, chill out, man. Just say your piece. No need to flip the hell out."

I take several deep breaths as I try to cool my blistering resentment. My eyes skitter over to the menu board near the counter where you place your order. A cold beer would really take the edge off about now.

Trent clears his throat and my eyes fly back to his.

"I'm seeing a therapist. He's helping me with my recovery."

He nods slightly in approval. It's just enough of a push that I continue.

"Anyway, he thinks that I need to work on my relationship with you—that we need to spend some time together."

He glances out the window for a moment as he says, "I'm a busy guy."

My heart explodes furiously in my chest. "Busy? Really, Trent? Too fucking busy for your own brother? You're not too busy to be a Big Brother at the Salvation Army. How about you find some time to be a 'big brother' to your own flesh and blood!"

A deep voice calls out from the kitchen and a burly man—clearly the cook based on his stained, greasy shirt—steps out into the dining room. "You two having a problem over there?"

Trent, ever the gentleman, stands from his seat and strides over to the cook. I palm my cheeks as the two men speak in hushed whispers. Moments later, he comes back carrying two glasses of Pepsi.

"I got The Hawaiian. Hope that's okay."

Lifting my eyes, I smile crookedly at him as he slides back into the booth. Mom used to flip out when we ordered The Hawaiian because she hated the smell of cooked pineapple. It became our favorite and we loved the disgusted expression on her face every time we got it. The Hawaiian became our own little joke, a small way we'd terrorize our mother—typical of preteen boys. Even Dad would eat it and then try to kiss her afterwards.

Maybe Trent's trying here.

"You should call Mom and invite her," I joke.

He rewards me with a genuine, full-on grin. "I'll bring her some leftovers."

We both chuckle for a moment before becoming serious again.

"Trent, why do you hate me?"

There. I said it. What's been on my mind pretty much ever since the day he turned thirteen. We went from being brothers to archnemeses.

He groans but meets my stare. "I don't hate you. I hate some of the things you do, but I don't hate you."

"Then why do you treat me like shit? Why am I the fucking black sheep of the family?" My voice is rising again—I'm not sure I can control the fury threatening to explode out of me.

Shaking his head, he takes a sip of his soda before answering me. His demeanor is calm and it pisses me right the fuck off. "Because, Thad, it's like you enjoy stirring shit up wherever you go. You're always doing the worst possible crap to infuriate Mom. Honestly, it's annoying. Man the fuck up already and become an adult."

I'm about three seconds from throwing my Pepsi at him. "Become an adult? Trent, I'm a recovering addict. It has nothing to do with 'manning up.' Did it ever occur to you that, because of the bullshit ways you and Mom treated me, I became an addict in the first place?"

My muscles are quivering with the need to hit something—*someone*. I angrily clench my teeth together and fist my hands in my lap.

It's his turn to become irritated and he flails his arms in the air. "Who do you think has worked his entire life to be fucking perfect to get her off your ass in the first place? Me. When you were getting high in high school with your friends, I was working my ass off so Mom would lay off yours. I thought that, if I did well, she'd leave you the hell alone. What else was I supposed to do, Thad? Become a fuckup too? Someone had to grow up and take charge. That someone was me!" His nostrils are flaring furiously and his face has turned bright red.

I remember seeing this same look many times as a teenager—it was the look he'd get right before he'd beat my ass in the yard for throwing eggs at the neighbor's garage door or tackle me in the living room for sneaking shots of bourbon from our parents' liquor cabinet.

"Why couldn't you have just been my brother? Why'd you have to make everything a fucking competition—competition that I was always destined to lose?" My voice has lost its strength and my chest feels tight. I could really go for that fucking beer right now.

"I'm sorry."

I raise an eyebrow at him in surprise. "Come again?"

"I said I'm sorry, okay? Yes, there were times I knew it was wrong. What started as a need to protect you soon became a need to be in the spotlight. The more positive attention I got from Mom, the more I craved it. The more I watched her treat you badly, the more I knew I didn't want to be in your shoes. I did everything to please her, Thad. I did it at your expense and I'm sorry."

My jaw must be on the floor at this point because I wasn't expecting a willing apology. As my throat constricts with emotion, I swallow down the pussy feeling to cry. "I need you, Trent. I need my fucking brother. Enemies? I have plenty—don't need any more. We were born to be on the same side. That's what brothers are—lifelong friends."

He nods. "I want to be there for you, man. I'll try to do better. I promise."

For some reason, I believe his promise. Maybe we can find a way to become friends. I just hope he doesn't let me down—*again*.

"Oh." He narrows his eyes at me. "I'll still always win when it comes to one particular thing."

My body burns with outrage because he will never win over Opal. *Ever.* She's mine. I'm about to throttle his ass when he chuckles and nods over to the arcade games.

Oh.

All fury dissipates as booming laughter bursts from me. "In your dreams, big bro," I smirk. "Prepare to be dominated!"

After a kicking his ass on our favorite game and filling our bellies with Mom's "favorite" pizza, we sit back and chat easily about lighter subjects. Neither of us mentions Opal. He doesn't know that we're seeing each other and I don't see any reason in dropping that bomb while things are going so well.

His phone chimes and he excuses himself to answer an important e-mail to a client. After he sets his phone back on the table, he looks up at me in question. "Are you going to Mom's benefit party tomorrow night?"

A groan escapes me before I can stop it. "Do I have to?"

He cocks up an eyebrow. "I thought you were told by your shrink that you needed to work on your relationships. Coming to Mom's benefit would be a step in the right direction. I've got your back."

I sigh in relief. "Yeah, okay. I'll go. But you better fucking keep her claws out of me—I'm not strong enough for that shit."

He nods his promise before sliding out of the booth. "I need to take a piss before I go back to the office. Lunch is on me." He grins and tosses me his wallet before striding off toward the back.

I wave the lady from the cash register over and hand her a wad of cash from my wallet. *Lunch is on me, big bro.*

Curiosity gets the better of me and I flip open his wallet. I'm shocked to find a tattered picture of him and that chick he used to date—the one he truly liked. Carmen? Cara? Candace? Shit. I was so fucked up the few times I met her that I can't even remember her fucking name. Slapping the wallet closed, I toss it back over to his side of the table.

When his phone chimes, I nosily snatch it up. A text from Mom.

Mom: Are you bringing a plus-one? Anna will be there.

Anna?
I type back as Trent.

Trent: Is Anna hot? You should hook us up. Thad is coming and bringing a plus-one.

The response is immediate.

Mom: Son, you've met her a million times. What's gotten into you? I've tried setting you two up on numerous occasions. I'm glad you're finally coming around though. As for your brother, make sure that he and his date dress accordingly. I don't want to be embarrassed in front of my colleagues.

A fucking embarrassment. That's all I am to her. I don't reward her with a response and instead look at his last texts. My eyes widen when I see a conversation between him and Opal.

Trent: Opal, I'm so sorry. I need to see you again.

Opal: Let's meet for lunch tomorrow. Pick me up at noon.

What in the ever-loving fuck? I check the time stamp—this was from this morning! I slide his phone across the table back to his seat and pull mine out.

Me: I want to take you to lunch tomorrow. Pick you up at noon?

She responds quickly.

Opal: That's sweet but I've been piled high with work stuff…tomorrow's just not a good day for lunch. Sorry!

Unfuckingreal!

I thought she was done with my brother. Why in the fuck is she having a secret lunch date with him? She didn't get fucked over enough the first time by him—she needs a second helping?

"Okay, little bro. Lunch was fun, but I really do have to get back. I have a client coming in at two and—" he rambles, but I interrupt him and stand abruptly from the booth.

"She's mine! You don't even fucking like her!" I spit out at him and advance until my chest touches his.

"What the fuck is your problem, Thad?" he demands in confusion.

At this point, our noses are practically touching. Then he scoops up his wallet and phone before storming from the restaurant. I must be a fucking embarrassment to him as well. After stalking after him, I grab his shoulder and spin him toward me once we're outside in the warm May air.

"Stay away from her!" Spittle sprays out as I vehemently lash out my warning. My chest heaves and I tighten my fists.

"Away from who?" he asks innocently. Innocent my fucking ass!

"Opal!"

He glares at me. "She's not yours."

"The hell she's not! I fucking rescued her ass from your apartment. You slept with her and treated her like a piece of garbage. She's not yours—she's mine!" I snarl.

He winces at my words, but anger builds within him and his face turns bright red. "Opal's a good girl."

"I know, and you need to stay the fuck away from her," I warn loudly.

Several people walk past us quickly and eyeball us as if we've lost our mind but sidestep around us as not to get in the middle of our squabble.

"No, Thad," he growls. "You need to stay the fuck away from her. She doesn't need someone like you in her life."

I fucking explode and haul off to punch him in his face, but he dodges me. "Motherfucker!"

"That"—he points to me angrily—"proves my point. You're a fucking train wreck waiting to happen. Do you really want to take her down with you? Get a clue, man. Like I said before, grow up and man the fuck up. I'm out."

His words cut me to my core. Helplessly, I watch him stride away from me.

Me.

The fucking embarrassment.

The train wreck.

Chapter EIGHTEEN

Opal

I lied to him.

What kind of person am I?

A knock sounds on my apartment door, so I tug my T-shirt over my head on the way to the door. After work, I rushed home to change before tonight's dinner at Olive's. Thad never responded to my text earlier, so I worried all day that maybe he'd forget about our plans this evening.

Why didn't I just tell him the truth?

I reach the door and exhale heavily before plastering on a fake smile. When I open the door, my knees buckle. God, he's so fucking hot.

He's freshly showered, and his longish, chestnut hair is styled haphazardly all over his head. His green eyes are filled with heat but not lust. Instantly, guilt consumes me.

He knows.

"Hi," I squeak out. I want to look away from his piercing glare, but I can't. He's too delicious for me to not look at him.

My eyes travel down his strong nose down to his lips, which are pursed together in a firm line. His jaw clenches every few seconds. I can tell he's shaved his face—his normal scruffy look has been replaced by a clean-cut one. He's sporting a navy, button-up dress shirt over a white T-shirt. I smile when I see that he's wearing one of his signature pair of holey jeans and his tattered Doc Martens.

"O." His voice carries a hint of accusation, and I try not cringe.

When he looks past me into the kitchen, he grinds his teeth together. He's pissed.

"I lied," I blurt out as tears fill my eyes.

His emerald eyes darken at my admission. "About?"

I whimper and advance toward him, but he stumbles backwards as if I'm carrying the black fucking plague.

"Don't," he instructs firmly.

The tears spill over and a sob chokes me. I reach a hand in the direction of him, but he eyes it as if it's poison. I drop it and mutter out his name.

"Thad."

"I won't be played, Opal."

I wince. He hardly ever calls me Opal—I'm his O!

"I'm not playing you! I want you—not him!"

A growl rumbles in his chest and he advances on me like a lion stalking his prey. "Then why did you lie about having lunch with him tomorrow?"

My heart patters along. I didn't tell him the truth because it was supposed to be a quick, painless lunch to tell Trent that I was done chasing him. I knew it would hurt Thad, so I didn't even mention it.

"I did it for us!" I hiss as he closes in on me.

My entire body flushes with heat at his nearness. Will it always be this way when I'm around him—with my body out-of-control wild for him?

"Fucking my brother a second time to see if the first go-round was a *mistake*? How is that for US?!" His chest bumps mine and he glares down at me.

I know he's angry, but I'm not afraid of him. He'd never hurt me in a million years—no matter how pissed he is at me.

I slide my hands around his waist and hug him to me. Tension immediately leaves his body, but he doesn't reciprocate. Tilting my head upwards, I look into his pained eyes.

I did this to him.

His eyes leave mine and flit back over to my kitchen.

"I wasn't going to fuck him, Thad. I was going to let him apologize for 'that' night and then I was going to tell him I was seeing you. End of story. I shouldn't have lied about it and I'm sorry."

He groans and tangles his hand in my hair. Dragging his eyes from the kitchen, he peers back down at me. The fury has left him and his expression is almost embarrassed.

"O," he whispers and nudges my nose with his, "I'm goddamn losing my mind today. I feel like getting fucked up."

I can tell that he's horrified to admit such a thing because he shamefully squeezes his eyes shut. Hugging him tighter to me, I lift on my toes and kiss his lips hard.

"Fuck me, Thad," I order heatedly. "Fuck me hard. Use me so you don't think about using anything else. I'll be your drug, baby."

His eyes fly open and he scowls at me. I don't cower under his gaze. In fact, it's hot as hell and I'm wet just from imagining him taking me roughly.

"Are you sure about this, sugar?" he questions with a growl from deep in his throat.

When I nod, his hand tightens in my hair, pulling my head backwards. The exposed flesh on my neck is where he attacks first. His lips are on my neck in an instant, nipping and sucking hard. A needful moan leaves my throat and echoes through my apartment.

"Take me, Thad," I beg.

And boy, does he take me.

My whole world spins as he flips me over his shoulder. He ignores my squeal of surprise and kicks the door closed. As he stalks into my bedroom, I bounce against his chiseled back. Panic momentarily fills me as thoughts of Drake peek from their carefully locked-away chamber in my mind.

Get the fuck out of my head, Drake!

When we make it to my bed, Thad drops me down onto my back and pounces on me. His lips and teeth taste and nip at my neck again. Once I spread my legs around his hips, he grinds his hardness against my throbbing center and I moan.

"Goddamn it, I need to be inside you."

"Then get rid of your clothes, lover boy," I taunt.

Tearing off me, he sits up and begins yanking off his clothes. His body is amazing—fucking amazing. His chest ripples with every movement, and I'm reminded that I still want to know more about those tattoos on his chest. Once he's completely naked, he sets to undressing me frantically. By the time he's rolled on the condom and is between my legs, my body is practically quivering desperately for him.

He descends upon me and grabs each of my wrists. Needing for him to be inside me already, I writhe beneath him. Without words, he understands what I want. Inch by inch, his cock slowly fills me, and I lift my hips to urge him all the way in. When he's completely seated inside me, he pushes my hands above my head and holds them together with one hand. Nerves immediately cause my body to quake.

"Thad." My voice is off—*unrecognizable.*

"You're not getting away, princess." His lips softly press against mine as he thrusts into me.

And.

I.

Fucking.

Lose.

It.

"You're not getting away, princess," Drake taunts hatefully.

Tears angrily roll down my cheeks. I will not beg—he gets off on begging. Instead, I glower at him.

"I hate you," I seethe between gritted teeth.

He clicks his tongue in admonishment. "You'll learn to love me, Olive."

My eyes clamp shut. This man is demented. I knew it the night I lost my virginity against my will that first night. Now, I'm used to his psychotic ass.

"Opal, asshole." Opening my eyes again, I spit in his face.

With his free hand, he forcefully grabs hold of my chin so I can't look away from him. "Olive, you're such a naughty bitch. I think I need to remind you who's the fucking boss around here!"

I cry out when he slaps me hard enough to see stars. Big, ugly fucking stars.

"I'll kill you one day," I promise.

He chuckles darkly. I'm not sure why I am poking the bear, but I do it anyway. I've had enough.

"Not if I kill you first," he growls.

Pain slices through my core as he takes me hard. Again.

"O!" Thad screams, shaking me wildly from my daytime nightmare.

I blink several times in confusion but soon realize that it was only a memory. *A very bad memory.* Thad, even having angry sex, is still a beautiful, loving soul. I couldn't be afraid of him if I tried. It's quite the opposite with him. I can't get enough.

"What the hell just happened?" he demands. He's still inside me, but he's no longer hard. His eyes are wild as he searches mine for answers.

"I had a flashback." Thoughts of Drake still linger and I burst into tears. I'm safe now. That rat bastard was put away years ago.

Thad brings a hand to my cheek and kisses my nose. "Baby, please tell me what just happened."

I can't stop crying, but I don't want to lose the physical and emotional connection with the man on top of me. "Make love to me. I'll tell you after."

He frowns down at me—his face wars between scrambling off me and granting me my wish.

"Please," I whisper and peck his lips. "I need this."

His eyes close, but when I kiss him harder, he parts his mouth open and meets my kisses. Within seconds, his cock is erect again inside me.

"Make love to me." This time, my order is heeded as he begins sliding in and out of me.

In this moment, it's not about getting off or fucking. It's about making new memories—writing over old ones.

"God, I don't understand you. You're so goddamn addicting, O," he murmurs against my lips.

My body tightens as it reaches for an orgasm on the horizon. With each deep thrust of him into me, I get closer and closer. Sweat perspires between our chests as we both quiver in anticipation of our ecstasy.

"You don't have to understand me—just be with me."

He nods against my lips and grunts. His body slaps against mine pound after pound and echoes throughout the room. *God, I'm so close to losing control.*

Pressing my eyes closed, I give in to my climax. This time, bright, beautiful stars sparkle before me. Big, beautiful fucking stars.

"Yes, Thad!" I cry out.

He moans into my mouth as I feel his dick throb within me. When he empties himself into me, he sits up on his elbows and regards me seriously.

"Now." Not a question but an order.

I comply. Not because I have to, but because I want to.

"When I was eighteen, I moved in with a man. His name was Drake. He was a very bad man, Thad."

He tenses and his gaze becomes furious.

I sigh raggedly but continue. "He was a photographer who showed up on my doorstep to recruit me to model. God, I was so fucking naïve. I packed my shit and left without a glance back."

"Continue." His body is shaking. He knows that whatever I have to tell him will be ugly.

"At first, things were great. He was nice to me and I even got to model a little. I had my own room in his apartment. Things were fine. Well, they were fine until I was hunting for a stamp and went into his office. He told me never to go in there." I bite my lip and whine, "I just needed one stamp to mail my mother a letter. *One fucking stamp.*"

Tears burn a trail down my cheeks as I silently cry.

He dips his lips down to mine and kisses me supportively.

"And then I saw it. I saw the fucking shrine!" My voice is shrill as I remember that night. It was awful. Every single square inch of that room had a picture of my sister stapled to the wall. I was horrified.

"What shrine?" he asks against my lips.

"The shrine of her! My sister!" My body shivers as I recall how I felt when I discovered it. There were hundreds of photos of her. It was bizarre. He was a fucking stalker.

"Holy shit," he mutters and lifts up to look into my eyes. Concern paints his face, and I'm thankful—thankful to unload this story on someone.

"Exactly. So I storm into the living room, where he's watching football, and lay into him. Seconds tick by—maybe minutes—before he calmly stands. The calm was brief before the storm, and what a fucking storm he made. That night, I lost my virginity. Not by my choice," I sob loudly.

"I'll kill him," he whispers and gently kisses me again.

I chuckle darkly. "I'll get to him first."

The moments trickle by while we stare at one another.

"Is he in jail?"

"Yep."

"You're safe now, O."

"I'll be safe when I spit on his grave."

More moments pass.

"How'd you get away?" he asks finally.

I swallow and suppress a shiver. "One night, he got wasted and left his phone by the bed. That night was more of the same—sex and beatings. He'd fuck me as I had to stare at the tattoo of my sister's name on his chest. That shit does stuff to your head."

"God, I am so sorry," he mumbles.

"After he fell asleep, I called Momma and begged for her to get ahold of Olive. Bray and Jackson came to my aid. He's in jail now, but those memories resurface at times."

"I'll keep you safe. Always, O." His promise seeps into my soul, and I know without a shadow of a doubt that he means it.

Chapter
NINETEEN

Thad

Her hand feels small and fragile in mine as she guides me down the hallway of a very posh-looking building toward her sister's loft. Earlier, she unloaded one hell of a story on me. So much more makes sense with Opal now. Her decision to run off with Drake had been a terrible lapse of judgment, and she's spent the past several years doing everything in her power to not to do anything like that ever again.

That's how she became fixated on Trent. It stings a little that, in the beginning of our union, she was apprehensive to jump in with both feet with me. She's somehow lumped me into the same category as Drake.

A mistake.

"They're going to love you," she promises and plants a kiss on my cheek when we stop in front of a door at the end of the hallway.

I'll prove to her that I'm not some mistake. I'm not a disaster in her life like Drake was.

"You're the only one who matters," I tell her softly and hug her to me.

She pulls away with a grin and turns the knob on the door, letting us inside. The way she just walks into her sister's loft unnerves me because, in my family, you would never do such a thing. Mom has her order—*her rules*—and knocking before entering is one of them.

What sounds like a herd of elephants storming toward us ends up just being two little girls who attack Opal as she enters, nearly slamming her to her ass. "Aunt Opie! Aunt Opie!" they both squeal in such a high pitch that I'm surprised the huge windows along the far wall of the space don't explode.

"Abby! Mia! I missed you too!" she laughs and hugs them tight.

The girls look nothing alike. Even though they are about the same age—four, maybe five—their looks are completely different. One of the girls has long, dark hair, fair skin, and piercing, brown eyes. The other has wavy, coffee-colored hair, pale-brown eyes, and tan skin—possibly the exotic combination of a biracial couple.

"Thad, this is my niece, Abby," Opal says, introducing me to the darker-skinned girl.

I squat down and offer my hand to shake, but she launches herself at me, hugging me around my neck instead. Both girls giggle when I fall backwards and land on my ass with an "Oof!"

Abby finally releases me and points to the other little girl. "This is Mia. She's my best friend. We both love Frozen. She likes to play Queen Elsa and I always pretend to be Anna. Do you have a puppy? Daddy won't let me get a puppy because he said we don't have a yard for it to play in. Will you buy me a yard for Christmas so Daddy can get me a puppy? Are you going to be my uncle? I want you to be my uncle. Why did you color on your neck? Did you draw a picture of your house?"

The little girl excitedly rambles on and on, never giving me a chance to answer her questions. Opal can't stop laughing as Abby assaults me with questions while I get back to my feet. Finally, the one named Mia steps in to save me.

"Abby," she sasses with her nose in the air. "He can't hear you and he can't speak. Let's go play Barbie dolls. My Barbie is going to Princeton like Daddy."

I widen my eyes in disbelief at her snootiness, shake off the Princeton reminder—a reminder of my brother—and send a frazzled glance over to Opal. She shrugs off the children's comments and questions with a smile as if she's used to them.

As we round the corner of the hallway, we find two women sitting on the sofa with tears in their eyes. When they see us, they burst out laughing. I recognize the pretty blonde as Andi from Dr. Sweeney's. The other one stands and swipes at her cheek.

"Sorry, Thad. The girls are nuts. I'm Olive, Opal's sister," she chuckles.

I stride over and shake her hand. She and Opal look very different. Olive looks exactly like her daughter—exotic.

"Nice to meet you. I'm crazy about your sister," I grin at her.

Andi stands and runs over to envelop me in her signature miniature bear hugs. "You're a keeper, Thad In My Pants."

When she releases me, Opal speaks up. "Where are the guys? Where's Pepper?"

Olive bends to pick up some coloring books and stacks them on the coffee table. "They went to get takeout. Pepper had to go with them because she's pregnant and nothing sounds good to her—like, ever. I'm sure she has them driving all over the Upper East Side looking for mashed potatoes and lo mien or something disgusting that only pregnant women find appetizing."

Opal and Olive smile, but Andi looks down at her feet with a frown. I recognize her pain. I'm about to ask her if she's okay when the front door bursts open and a flurry of commotion soon follows.

"Jordan, so help me… If she forgot my fortune cookie, you have to go back. I have been craving those damn things for a week now!" a pissed-off, attractive, pregnant brunette snaps as she wobbles in the door. It's clear she's about to pop out that kid any day.

"Babe, I'm sure it's in there. You reminded her, *dare I say*, fifteen times?" he questions with a grin as he looks over at me. I recognize him immediately. He's Trent's college buddy, and I've met him on a few occasions.

He waves to me in greeting as he ushers the pregnant one over to the kitchen table, where they begin pulling food out of bags in her search for her precious fortune cookie.

"It's not here!" she hisses dramatically and flails her arms in the air.

A tall, solid, blond man stalks up behind her and tickles her ribs.

144

She swings at him, but he easily dodges her pregnant ass. "Bray, so help me, if I have this baby on your hardwoods, I will kill you."

He laughs and holds his hand out to her. When she snatches an empty fortune cookie wrapper out of his hands, I think he may have started the World War III.

"You ate my fortune cookie, you motherfucker!"

We're all laughing, even Jordan, when Bray points to Andi's brooding asshole of a husband and says, "There were two, Pepper. Chill your shit. Jackson's keeping it safe for you."

Her relief is palpable as she holds out her hand expectantly to Jackson. He cocks a dark eyebrow at her before handing her another empty wrapper. Those two are up to some shit—both of them dead set on terrorizing her. When she realizes what he's done, the poor girl turns so red that I think she might give herself an aneurism.

"I fucking hate you two! Jordan, take me back to Pei Wei."

Jackson laughs his ass off as he begins pulling a shitload of fortune cookies from another bag and tossing them at her one at a time.

Jordan shakes his head and bites back a laugh as he picks them up off the floor and sets them on the table. "Leave my wife alone, Jackie. I don't want to have to kick your ass, because then Mom will kick mine."

I try to ignore the pang of jealousy in my chest. Those two men clearly have a great relationship—one that brothers are supposed to have. They probably have a normal mother too.

"Guys, this is Thad," Olive says, finally introducing me to the group.

As if realizing for the first time that I'm here, Bray's and Jackson's demeanors change. Both men square their shoulders and glare at me.

What the fuck did I do?

"I remember you. Keep your hands off my wife," Jackson snips out and stalks over to Andi. When he hugs her possessively, I refrain from rolling my eyes.

If he knew that, moments before, I hugged her, we might be rolling around on the floor while he tried to beat my ass.

Opal comes around to my side and slides an arm around my hip. "Be nice to my boyfriend, punk." She's trying to lighten the air, but I bristle at her having to protect me from the big, bad Jackson.

"What are your intentions with my sister?" Bray demands.

Both Olive and Opal shout, "Bray!" at the same time. My body tenses because I feel like I'm on the other end of the fucking firing squad.

I meet his challenging glare. "I care about, O." The firm, unwavering tone of my voice seems to cause him to relax a bit.

"Good, because I wouldn't want to have to kill you." I think he's joking, but I hear the warning loud and clear. He loves her dearly and protects her as if she's his flesh and blood.

"I can respect that," I tell him honestly.

Once he nods, the tension in the room dies down. The women flurry over to the table and start pulling food from bags and sorting it all.

The pregnant one, Pepper, eyes me with a disdainfully arched chestnut eyebrow. She briefly glances at the tattoo on my neck, the one Abby thought I'd drawn, that peeks just above my collar of my shirt. When she looks back up at me, she scowls. Then she mouths, "I'm watching you," and, in a creepy-as-fuck move, does a two-finger action as she points to her eyes and then over at me.

I can handle Bray and Jackson with their alpha protectiveness. But Pepper? Her pregnant hormones coupled with the feral look in her eyes makes her unpredictable. Pepper scares the shit out of me.

During dinner, we all soon fall into comfortable conversation. I only have to dodge the warning glares of Pepper the Viper a couple of times, and the veins in Jackson's neck only stand out once when I high-five Andi after she says that the Harry Potter and the Sorcerer's Stone movie is better than the book.

We're just finishing up dinner when Olive stands. "Girls, if you're all through, you can go play."

The girls squeal as they leave the dinner table, and we all watch them run off before our attention is back on Olive. Opal squeezes my hand under the table. She seems slightly nervous about whatever Olive has to say. I return the gesture and quickly kiss her on the cheek.

"I have an announcement," Olive breathes out anxiously. "Jo has once again asked me to purchase the firing range so that she can retire."

I sneak a glance over at Opal and she smiles.

"But I declined her once and for all. The reason is that we've decided to expand our family." She grins and looks over at Pepper, who nods supportively. "We've been on a list for an intercountry adoption and have finally been approved. Next month, we'll be travelling to Haiti to meet Astryd, a sweet, two-year-old orphan girl."

Opal gasps in surprise. "Olive, that's great news. Congratulations!"

My eyes flit over to Andi, whose face is ashen. Her long, blond hair hangs around her face as she stares into her lap.

"I need to go to the restroom," she says suddenly and nearly knocks her chair over when she all but runs from the table.

Everyone is chattering happily to Olive and Bray, but my eyes follow the sad woman who is slipping into the bathroom. I look over at Jackson, expecting him to go after her, but he's launched into a Twenty Questions marathon as he drills Bray for answers about the adoption process. Finally, when I realize that nobody seems to care about what happened to Andi, I stand. I'm ignored as I excuse myself and stride over to the bathroom.

When I reach the door, I hear sniffling on the other side. I tap the door with my knuckle.

"You okay in there?"

A bitter laugh echoes in the bathroom. "Peachy."

Rolling my eyes, I turn the knob and discover that it's unlocked. I push inside and see Andi's red, tear-stained face fixated on her purse as she rummages around in it, looking for something. Her hands find purchase on a prescription pill bottle, and it rattles as she opens it with shaky hands. The bottle slips from her grasp and the container hits the floor, spilling the pills everywhere.

"Shit!" she hisses as she drops to her knees to pick them up.

Scooting inside, I close the door behind me and kneel down in front of her to help her pick them up. When I grab up a handful, I open my palm. *Valium.* I knew what they were the moment I saw the engraved V and the light-blue color of the pill. The urge to pocket the handful in my hand while she's distracted as she frantically picks them up is strong, but I refrain and continue helping her gather them. This chick needs her meds.

"Want to explain the meltdown?" I question as I hold out my hand to her.

She collects the pills from my palm and drops them into the bottle before looking up at me. Her eyes are uncontrolled as she sets one of the pills in the back of her throat and swallows it down dry. A bizarre laugh escapes her.

"Since you asked, *Dr. Sweeney*, let me tell you. I melted down because I'm sick and fucking tired of the fact that I can't have kids always being shoved down my throat. It's irrational, I know. I love those women in there—they're two of my best friends. But every single day I see them, I'm reminded that they can have what I want. It comes easy to them. For me, it's a fucking nightmare." Her body trembles and I have the urge to hug her.

"Do you want me to get Jackson?" I ask gently, placing a comforting hand on her shoulder.

She shakes her head fervently. "No. He's had enough of it. I can't keep blowing up on him every time I see a stroller or a fucking Pampers commercial. I'm choosing my battles, and the less I have to smother him with, the better. I don't want him to resent me."

Her entire body is still shaking as she kneels on the floor. Leaning forward, I do what feels right. *I hug her.* The anxiety and distress immediately evaporate as she lets me embrace her. As I hold her, she sobs loudly into my chest.

"Andi, it will be okay. Things will work out. I'm here if you ever need to talk. I understand about trying to hide your crazy." I grin and squeeze her tighter.

Her sobs become laughs, and I stroke her hair in a comforting move. "Thank you, Thad. Sorry to unload. I'm glad Opal has you. She's special, but then again, so are you."

We're about to break apart from our hug when the bathroom door flies open. A pissed-off Jackson stands over us, hands on hips. Anger at our physical connection ripples from him and the bathroom suddenly feels impossibly smaller.

"What the fuck are you doing with my wife?" he snaps.

Before either one of us can explain, he fists the back of my shirt and hauls me to my feet. I'm shoved out of the bathroom and land with a thud on my ass on the hardwood floors for the second time tonight. They really need carpet. Then the bathroom door slams closed behind him.

"I think they like you," a familiar voice teases.

I look up to see an amused Opal standing over me with her hand stretched toward me. "You're right. Especially Jackson. Maybe I should go in there and ask him if he wants to see a movie later." My voice drips with sarcasm.

I take her hand and we both grin as she helps me up. Then she stands on her toes and kisses my nose.

"Jackson will have to take a rain check," she tells me saucily, "Tonight, you're mine."

Every night, you're mine, O.

Chapter TWENTY

Opal

"Want to be my date tomorrow night for my mom's benefit?" Thad asks with a lopsided grin as he leans against the other mailboxes in my apartment building, watching me pull my mail. He took off the dress shirt and left it in his car before we got out, and now, I'm having trouble keeping my eyes off his toned chest, which is stretching his white T-shirt.

I glance over the Soundgarden emblem on his shirt before skirting my eyes back to his amused green ones. "Not really," I laugh. It's the truth. If I never see that vile woman again, it will be too soon.

He reaches over and tickles me on the ribs. "You're going, woman."

I squeal and drop the wad of mail onto the floor as I jerk away from his punishing fingers. "Asshole," I tell him and good-naturedly stick my tongue out at him.

He winks, which effectively warms my insides, as he drops to one knee to retrieve the mail. Thad on one knee is a look any woman could get used to. His demeanor changes from playful to serious as he snatches up an envelope and reads the front.

My heart pounds as I reach for it, but he jerks it away. Quickly, he scoops up the mail and stands. The letter is practically crumpled in his fist—and he's pissed.

"Let's get upstairs. Now," he growls.

"What is it?" I question, but it goes unanswered as he stalks over to the opening elevator to keep it from closing. I follow him on and cross my arms.

He pushes the button to my floor but doesn't look over at me. Leaning forward, I try to catch a peek at what has his panties in a wad, but he moves it to his side, out of my line of sight.

When the doors open, he storms out and takes long strides to my apartment door. I hurriedly follow after him. My fingers are shaking, causing the keys to jingle as I nervously try to unlock the door and get us inside. Once I get the door open and we make into my entryway, he drops the mail—*all but the letter*—and flips the deadbolt.

The only light in my dark apartment comes from the lamp beside the couch that stays on as we enter.

"We'll read this together. No matter what, I'm here for you. Always," he promises as he takes hold of my elbow and guides me over to my sofa.

Everything about the way he's acting is scaring the shit out of me. Something on that letter has him worried. I'm terrified about what it could be as he sits and pulls me with him into his lap. Gently, I take the semi-crumpled letter from his fist.

No air.

Maybe it's just informational.

Fuck!

City of New York Department of Corrections Victim Services blazes boldly in blue type across the front of the letter. My fingers are in autopilot as I tear open the letter. Four years ago, when Drake went away to prison, I filed a request for notification of release. He was supposed to serve way more time than four years. This can't pertain to his release. It. Just. Can't.

May 8ᵗʰ, 2014
City of New York Department of Corrections
Victim Services
RE: Prisoner Drake Edmond Brinkley

151

Dear Ms. Opal E. Redding,

The City of New York has honored your request for notification of prisoner release. Prisoner Drake Edmond Brinkley has been approved for early parole and is scheduled for release on the twenty-first of May, two thousand and fourteen.

As a victim of sexual and domestic crimes, you have certain rights. Your rights include a notification of released prisoner address and occupation. Mr. Brinkley will be residing in a home for reformed men in Brooklyn. The address is posted below. Additionally, his new occupation is an overnight stocking clerk at the Homeland grocery store also in Brooklyn. This address is posted below as well. His address is in compliance with the law and does not violate your restraining order.

The City of New York Department of Corrections has deemed Mr. Brinkley fit to rejoin society. They have determined that he is rehabilitated and reformed.

If you have any other questions about this letter, please contact us via the number below.

Sincerely,
George Cottins
Warden

Two weeks. In two fucking weeks, my nightmare will be released. The letter falls to my lap and I feel Thad wrap his arms around me, pulling me to him.

"I'll keep you safe," he promises, his lips pressed into my hair.

I shiver in his arms. When it comes to Drake, I'll only feel safe when he's dead. Sighing, I climb off Thad to make a call I dread making. The call to Olive. Her happy day will be ruined.

Fuck Drake.

"Do you have any birthmarks?" Thad asks, breaking our silence, as he traces a circle on my breast through my shirt.

After an emotional phone call with Olive earlier, we crawled into my bed so he could hold me while I cried. The cries turned into hiccups, and eventually, I became quiet.

"No, do you?"

He chuckles, but the laughter is hollow—fake, even. "On my chest."

I watch him as he sits up and pulls his T-shirt off. For as many times as I've seen him naked, I've never properly inspected the artwork on his chest. He rolls onto his back so I can view him. Leaning up on my elbow on my side, I examine him, my eyes trailing each colored curve.

"Where is your birthmark?" I question. He said that he has one on his chest, but I can't find it because I'm distracted by the ink.

"The rock. The tattoo artist designed the artwork around my birthmark and included it as part of the design."

My eyes zero in on the huge, jagged "rock" that stretches across his breast bone. I'm drawn into the design—it's beautiful and horrifying at the same time. The original "rock" is the centerpiece and more tattooed rocks have been added all around it. From behind the rock, a tiger's paw with claws unsheathed reaches up toward his throat. The claws are what always peek from the top of his shirts. Below the rubble of the rocks are skulls and demons. It's sort of creepy.

I wonder what it means?

"You're the tiger. Rising above your demons?"

The pills.

The alcohol.

His addiction.

"Always. They're always pulling me down—they think I'm weak. I'm not, O. I am strong. I'll always claw my way to the surface. I will beat them." His voice is strong—so sure.

I believe him.

"Of course you will. I'll be there with you. Now that we have each other, we don't have to face anything alone." I lean over and kiss the rock in the center of his chest.

When my eyes find his, he's staring at me with an emotion I've not seen from him yet.

"What?" I ask with a smile.

He rolls us back over so that I'm pinned beneath him and his lips softly brush against mine. "You." He flashes one of his lopsided grins—the kind that always manages to set my heart in overdrive. A heat prickles across my flesh.

"Me?"

"Yep, you. Thanks for taking a chance on me. I know going after the tattooed, former rehab patient must have been hard for you with your issues. I'm so fucking glad that you opened yourself up to the spark that started the moment we laid eyes on each other. Now, that spark has become a blaze I never intend on letting die out. You're my person, O."

My breath rushes out as he crushes me with his body, kissing me hard. "You're my person too, Thad," I tell him between kisses.

Abruptly, he pulls away and my eyes fall to his glistening lips. God, he's so delicious.

"Tell me about the man who might be your dad."

I sigh because, even though I've told myself not to get my hopes up, they already are. I want Dr. Ellis to be my dad.

"Andi's doctor, turns out, knows my mother. Your mom and mine could have a contest to see who would win Mother of the Year. It would probably be a tie," I frown.

His brows drop as he lets my words soak in. "So your mom's an uncaring, selfish bitch."

My smile is fake. "Pretty much. Anyway, after some discussion, he thinks he's my father. In fact, this morning, I went down and did a paternity test. We'll have the results in a couple of days."

He slides his hand to cup my cheek and thumbs my skin along my cheekbone. "What do you want? Do you hope that this man is your father?"

Biting my lip, I nod reluctantly. "And that's the problem. He's so good—such a sweet, caring person in comparison to my mother. I just want one parent who loves me. That's *all* I want."

He smiles and kisses the tip of my nose. "O, it's okay to want that. I hope that he is your father."

Threading my fingers through his hair, I guide him to lie back down on my chest. My fingernails gently scratch his scalp and it earns me a pleasured groan.

"Tell me about the day you decided to go to rehab. What was the moment where you'd had enough?" My voice is soft with my question.

He tenses in my arms but finally releases a rush of breath. "Things had really been unravelling. Mom was continually on my case about going back to college and shit even though I was happy working for Griff. Dad and Trent were still too far up each other's asses to notice me. I'd taken to hanging with my best friend, Kurt, every night after work. Kurt really is a good guy, but he has no drive and is weak when it comes to the very vices I have trouble with. Anyway, I'd pass out all the time after a night of all sorts of experimental drugs. One particular morning, I woke up and once again had no recollection of the night before. I was naked between two chicks. One was my girlfriend at the time and the other was some random chick. I don't remember having sex with either of them. I had no idea the age of the one beside me. To this day, I'm not even sure if I used a condom. I'd been playing with fire and eventually was going to get burned."

He could have gotten a sexually transmitted disease.

He could have gotten someone pregnant.

He could have gone to jail for statutory rape.

"That morning, I crawled out of bed and drove myself straight to Mom's. She looked up a rehabilitation facility here in the city and dropped me off. I was tested for STDs, and thank fuck I was clean. I'm still unsure what happened that night. I haven't had the balls to ask Whitney or Kurt."

Whitney—his girlfriend. Just her name on his lips sends a burn of jealousy through my veins.

"I'm sorry, Thad," I whisper as I finger the hair on his head.

"Honestly, I don't want to know what happened now. I just want to focus on my future. My happiness—you, O."

He turns his head on my chest and begins kissing a trail down along my belly through my shirt. Much to my delight, he spends the rest of the night focusing on me, just like he promised.

Chapter
TWENTY
-ONE

Thad

Vibrations.

Over and over again.

What in the hell?

My eyes open, but it's still dark. I can hear Opal's soft breaths as she sleeps naked, curled around my own bare flesh. Her tits are pressed into my side and my dick hardens automatically. Unfortunately, the sound of repetitive vibrations jerks me from thoughts of continuing our love fest.

Sliding out of bed, careful not to wake her, I hunt for the noise. Within moments, I find the source—my phone in my pants pocket. I swipe it open to see several missed calls from Kurt. Pulling on my jeans, I slip barefoot and bare-chested out of Opal's room and into the living room. Like magnets, my feet carry me into the kitchen while I dial Kurt back. I lean my ass against the counter and stare up at the cabinet above the refrigerator while I wait for him to answer.

"T-t-had. G-get over here."

I fucking knew it. He's wasted and misses his party buddy. And it annoys me that he's calling me to join him.

"Dude, you know I don't do that shit anymore," I snap in a hushed whisper. Then, as my eyes flit back up to the cabinet, the realization hits me—I'll always struggle with my demons.

But I'm stronger than they are.

"No, m-man. It's Wh-Wh…" he trails off.

"Whitney?"

"Yesss. S-s-something's wr-wrong with her."

I may not want to party with them because of my recovery, but I can't sit back and not help them. Whitney has a tendency to overdo everything. There's no telling what she took and how much.

"I'll be right there," I promise and hang up.

Stalking back into Opal's room, I hunt around on the floor for my shirt, using the light from my phone. She's still sleeping peacefully.

Do I wake her to tell her where I'm going?

She'll just want to go with me—I know her.

Do I really want her to see the ugly part of my past? To see Whitney?

No.

I need to keep Opal in the present—in my future. She doesn't belong in my dirty past. I need to deal with this one on my own. So I throw on the rest of my clothes and sneak out the front door.

The ride to Kurt's in the middle of the night is a fairly traffic-free ride and quiet. My mind is on autopilot, and before I know it, I'm pushing open the door to his place.

All sorts of fucking commotion rings out from the bathroom. I storm over to it and my eyes widen at the sight. My mind has trouble comprehending what the fuck is really going on. All three of them—Whitney, Kurt, and Rhonda—are butt-ass naked and covered in red body paint. Rhonda has a bottle of bleach and is using a toothbrush to scrub the grout lines in the bathtub. Whitney is hunched over the toilet, puking. Kurt is fucking tweaking—every few minutes, he jerks his line of sight to the corner of the bathroom and mumbles something.

What a fucking joke—the whole lot of them. But two months ago, I *was* them.

"What happened?" I demand a little too loudly. My booming voice echoes in the bathroom and Rhonda screams.

"Thad! Are you hungry? Want me to cook you some eggs? Some

lasagna? Sushi? Do you want to do a line with us? Want me to paint your body? I'm really good at painting. I could paint a desert scene on your back. Do you want me to wash your hair? I washed Kurt's hair. Isn't it nice? I'm going to be his wife—wives wash their husbands' hair. Whitney loves you. You should love Whitney. Have you seen my cat? Here, kitty, kitty." Rhonda's arms flail while she chatters.

I look back at Kurt and he grins at me. He once again mouths, "Marriage material," to me and winks.

Shaking my head, I grab his bicep. "Come on, man. Time for bed. You too, Sparky," I tell Rhonda. As I half-drag him back to his room, a still-blabbing Rhonda follows after me. I ignore more of her statements and questions as I practically shove him into the bed.

"Have you been to Ellis Island? Oh my God! Let's go see the Statue of Liberty! Thad, can you take us on the Harley? I'll sit on Kurt's lap because I'm going to be his wife one day. Or maybe we could go to—"

Clutching her by the shoulders, I look her in her twitchy, blue eyes. "Maybe some other day after you've had a rest. I think you need to go lie down with your soon-to-be husband. Good wives do that sort of thing."

Her eyes widen and she grins knowingly at me. I don't have to ask her again before she does a running leap and attacks Kurt with hugs like a fucking spider monkey. Turning on my heel, I storm out of the room back toward Whitney.

She's still hunched over the commode. Her body no longer racks with shudders from heaving. Kneeling down beside her, I pull her long, blond locks back so I can see her face. She looks like fucking hell, especially now that I can see chunks of vomit all in her hair.

"You okay, Whit? Do you need to go to the hospital?"

She shakes her head vehemently. "No, but my skin itches. Get this shit off of me!" she hisses and begins clawing at the paint on her arms.

My eyes skip over to the shower and I groan because there's fucking bleach everywhere. I'll have to help her in Kurt's bathroom.

"Come on. I'll help you get cleaned up. Once you're settled on the couch, you need to get a good night's sleep. Tomorrow, you need to think about where the fuck your life is going."

As she bursts into tears, guilt consumes me. With a grumble, I help haul her to her feet. The girl is shaking like a leaf and can barely stand on her own two feet. Sliding my hand under her bare ass, I scoop her into my arms to carry her into the other bathroom. When she looks up at me with vacant, sad eyes, I have to look away. I recognize that look—I've seen it in my own eyes in the mirror before. Her arms slide around my neck and she buries her face into my chest, ruining my shirt with the red paint.

As we push back into Kurt's room, I have to quickly divert my eyes from the scene on the bed. They look creepy as hell as they fuck violently. Kurt's hands are on Rhonda's tits, squeezing while she rides him like he's a fucking wild bull, thrashing crazily. Because they are both red from head to toe, it looks like they're into some weird fetish shit.

I hurry past them and into the bathroom with Whitney in my arms. Slowly, I ease her down to the toilet and start the shower. How in the hell did I become their fucking babysitter? How in the hell did we survive before—when nobody was the sober one? It's amazing none of us ever died from an overdose.

"All right, Whitty. Into the shower," I instruct as I hold my hand out to her.

She eyes it tearfully and then looks back up at me. "You called me Witty. That's what you used to always call me when we had sex. You do love me—just like Rhonda said," she says hopefully.

I groan and shake my head. "Sorry, Whit. I don't love you. Sure, I care about you as a person, but I don't love you. Now get into the shower."

She begins bawling her eyes out but makes no moves to stand. Finally, I pull her to her feet again, but she's so unsteady that she can barely remain upright. When I sit her back down on the toilet, she claws at the painted flesh on her belly.

I'm going to have to get in with her. Fuck.

Tearing off my shirt and tossing it to the floor, I try not to think about what Opal would say. I know for a fact she'd be pissed as fuck. She just can't know.

Like she didn't tell you about lunch with Trent?

With a grumble, I push my jeans down and step out of them, but

I keep my boxers on. Once my socks are gone, I slide my hands under her arms and lift her. It's a challenge, but I finally manage to make it into the shower with her. The moment the warm water hits her back, she snakes her arms around my neck and hugs me.

Reaching down, I grab the bar of soap and begin washing her back and ass since she's holding on at the moment. The paint is crusted on, but it eventually starts to rinse away. I pull away, making sure she won't fall, and wash the rest of her. Her huge tits no longer turn me on—nothing about her is a turn-on anymore. In fact, she's disgusting and needs help. Not long ago, I was disgusting too.

I continue to scrub until I've managed to clean most of the paint off and wash the vomit out of her hair, I reach to turn off the water, but she tightens her hold around my neck.

"Thad, I need you," she whines.

Shaking my head, I start to push her away from me. One of her hands, lightning fast, slips down into my boxers and grips my dick.

"Let me get you hard, baby," she purrs.

"Whitney, no. Take your hand out of my shorts. Let's get you to bed."

She whimpers and reluctantly releases my flaccid cock. I'm so ready to be out of this fucking apartment and back with Opal. I quickly dry her off and wrap her in a towel. Turning away from her, I drop my boxers and proceed to redress.

"You're so hot," she whispers. She's always had a thing for my ass and right now it's in her face.

I roll my eyes and pull my jeans up, ending her show. After my clothes are on, I slide an arm around her and guide her out of the bathroom, past the now snoring freaky fuckers, and into the living room. Once we reach the couch, she crawls onto it and curls up. With a sigh, I snatch a blanket from the loveseat and cover her with it.

"Are you going to be okay?" I ask as I look her over. She hasn't thrown up anymore and she seems much more lucid now.

"Yes. Thank you, Thad."

I nod and start to leave. Before I get to the door, I stop and turn around. "Whit?"

"Yeah?"

"What happened that night? The night before I left for rehab?" I question softly.

She sits up and looks at me over the back of the couch. "With Brittney?"

I wince at the name. I hope to God that chick was not underage. "Yep. What did we do?"

She grins and cocks a brow up at me. "You were going to fuck both me and my cousin. I got jealous though and told her she could suck your dick but you were going to fuck me only."

My relief is loud and clear knowing I didn't sleep with the random girl.

"How old is Brittney? Did you and I use a condom?"

She laughs. "Brittney is the same age as me—twenty-four. And after she sucked you off, I watched her slide the condom on you. Why? Want to do it again?"

Shaking my head, I give her a slight wave. "Never."

I'm sitting in Dad's Lexus, which is parked on the street in front of my parents' home, at five fucking thirty in the morning. After I left Kurt's, I was going to slip back into Opal's apartment undetected, but several reasons stopped me. For one, I didn't have a key and had locked up behind me. I'd have had to call her or knock—and I wasn't at all prepared to explain where I'd been. The second reason was that my hair was soaking wet and disheveled on my head, I was no longer wearing underwear, and I had red paint under each of my fingernails. It looked bad. I need time to regroup before I see her again.

Sighing, I send her a text.

Me: Hey, babe. Left bright and early to grab a change of clothes and a shower at my parents'. Meeting a deliveryman at the property to receive the kitchen appliances. I'm still not sold on the idea of you having lunch with my brother. You're mine, not his, but I trust you.

I'll call you later.

It isn't a total lie. I do need a shower and a change of clothes. The deliveryman is bringing the appliances but not until noon. And she is mine, not his. What she doesn't know won't hurt her.

I climb out of the car and quietly slip into my parents' house. With it being an early Friday morning, they're both up. I try to sneak past the parlor, where they're having coffee and reading the news on their devices, but my mother's voice halts me.

"Thaddeus, darling, is that you?"

I am in no way, shape or form her darling. Groaning, I turn and step into the parlor.

"Hey. I have a full day of work today—just need to grab a quick shower before I head out," I tell her and then turn on my heel.

"It looks to me as if you've already had a shower. Where were you?" she questions.

Dad must be curious about our exchange because he has abandoned looking at what I know is the stock market to put his attention on me.

"Oh, uh, yeah. I just need to change. I was over at O—over at my girlfriend's house," I rush out. For some reason, I stop myself from verbalizing her name. It will only start a barrage of questions and accusations. She'll learn for herself of our relationship tonight at the benefit.

"Whitney? That trashy whore you used to date?"

I bristle at her remark. Whitney has problems, but calling her a trashy whore is unfair.

"No," I answer through gritted teeth.

"Good. I hope you are being responsible. The last thing this family needs is an unplanned pregnancy. Were you drinking?"

I shake my head. "No. Now, if you'll excuse me, I'll be in my room."

She holds up a slender hand to stop me. "Do not embarrass me tonight at the benefit. Make sure to tell your girlfriend to wear a cocktail dress. There's a suit in your closet upstairs. Tonight, a journalist from The New York Times will be interviewing our family for a huge piece they are doing on me and my practice. I'll expect you to be on your very best behavior. If they didn't know I had two children, I'd just ask you not to come at all. However, those nits know everything so now I must work with the hand I've been dealt."

Rage nearly explodes from me. "The hand you've been dealt? Do you realize you just referred to your son as a fucking nuisance?"

"That's enough, son," Dad snaps.

I'm surprised to see anything but an easygoing smile on his face. It only confirms that he isn't as innocent as I always thought. No, he just always chooses her over me—like Trent.

"It's the truth and you know it," I mumble.

When I look up at my mother, her smile is perfect—perfectly twisted. "See you at seven, darling."

Chapter TWENTY-TWO

Opal

"Are you sure everything's okay?" I ask Thad over the phone as I pick up my purse to leave for lunch. Trent texted moments before and said that he was in the parking garage of Compton Enterprises, waiting to take me to lunch.

"Everything's great. I can't wait to see you tonight. I'll pick you up at six thirty and then we can head to the event." His voice is overly perky. I don't trust the tone. Something is up.

Stopping in my tracks, I attempt to address the problem again. "Are you uncomfortable about my meeting him for lunch?"

He groans loudly. "Actually, yes, but I know it needs to be done."

I look down at my toes, which are peeking out of my sandals. "Thad, I don't have to go."

He instructs someone to move a ladder so the deliveryman can get past. "No, O, it's fine. Just don't fuck him."

His comment stings and I bite my lip.

"Shit. I'm sorry. Today is just a stressful day and I'm going on little sleep. I'll talk to you after work," he grumbles out his apology.

The dial tone lets me know that he hung up on me. Tears burn my eyes, but I quickly blink them away. He most certainly is not telling me something. I'll get to the bottom of it when I see him later.

I'm consumed by my thoughts the entire elevator ride down to the parking lot—so much so that, when the door opens and someone speaks to me, I nearly jump out of me skin.

"Thank you for meeting me," Trent's voice booms from behind me.

I sigh, relieved, because ever since last night, when I found out that Drake was going to be released soon, I've been jumpy. "It's no big deal."

His hand finds the small of my back and he guides me to his car. Then we both remain awkwardly quiet during the entire car ride to the Thai restaurant around the corner, the one I've been to several times with Bray and Olive. It isn't until we've both ordered and are sipping our sodas that either of us speaks again.

"So," I say softly as I roll the paper of the straw between my thumb and finger.

He groans. "So."

When my eyes find his, he appears to be completely uncomfortable, so I wait for him to continue.

"Opal, I'm sorry. We never should have slept together. We were drunk—it meant nothing." His voice is firm.

The old me would have been devastated at his words. The old me would have tried to convince him otherwise. This is the new me. The new me doesn't make dumb mistakes anymore.

"You're right, Trent. We're better off as friends. I went four years thinking it was you I wanted, but now, I know for a fact that it's not. I want someone else and I've never been surer."

He slides a hand through his perfect, blond hair, and I'm shocked to see him mess it up.

"My brother?"

The smile is already on my face before I can stop it. "Yes."

His eyes darken and his voice carries a protective edge—protective over me. "Opal, are you sure you want to get involved in that mess?"

Anger flares inside my chest. "That mess? Trent, that mess is your brother. I care for him deeply."

He shakes his head in frustration. "I didn't mean to insult you. It's just that I've known him my entire life. All he does is mess shit up. He's unpredictable. You're sweet, little Opal—the girl who has it all figured out. Has her life all planned out. You are going somewhere, unlike my brother. You have a chance at a full life. Don't let him and his inner demons drag you down with him."

My mind is flooded with images of Thad—the daily struggles he goes through are always so clearly written on his face. His green eyes constantly war between walking the line and giving in to his addictions. He's flawed, but I love that about him—I love that he's real and still strong despite those flaws.

"I'm sorry, but your brother is a good person no matter what you think you know about him. Yes, the man suffers with compulsions to use. Every day is a challenge for him, but he perseveres. I've seen the way he tries to hide the fact that he stares at my medicine cabinet, knowing a full bottle of painkillers sits on the other side. But he doesn't touch them. And when he did mess up and had a drink, he felt remorse. He wants to do better—he just needs proper support. Unfortunately, his own family has their heads so far up their asses that they can't extend a helping hand. Ever. How about being a loving big brother to him? He wants to connect with you. Why you would push out that tenderhearted, beautiful man is beyond me." There, I've said my piece. Trent cannot keep treating his brother like a pile of shit.

With a sigh, he squeezes his eyes shut before opening them up and glancing guiltily back over at me. "Shit. You're right. I'm sorry. I do want to help him—truly, I do. I just worry about you. I've looked after you and tried to be a good mentor to you while you were in school. You're like a little sister. I'm just looking out for you."

I suppress a shudder. We slept together and he thought of me as some kid the whole time. The old me would have keeled over with a heart attack at the humiliation. The new me swallows her pride and looks him dead in the eye.

"You don't have to worry about me, Trent. I'm a grown-ass woman. Your brother, on the other hand, could use your love and support. Promise me you'll try."

He nods without hesitation. "I'll try. I promise."

The server drops off our food, and after we dig in, Trent speaks again.

"Maybe we can be friends, Opal? I don't want to lose your friendship over this. I still care about what happens to you."

I smile. For once, the word doesn't make me cringe. "I'd like that."

The rest of our meal is light and we chat about what has never been a difficult topic for us—finance. When the server brings our check, he flips open his wallet and my eyes land on a picture safely protected by a plastic holder.

"Who's that?" I ask nosily. We're friends now, so I should know these things, and right now, I want to know about the cute woman with curly, blond hair in his wallet.

His face turns slightly red. "Cassidy. My ex-girlfriend."

My nose scrunches in confusion. Carrying around a picture of an ex seems odd.

"Why is she your ex?"

He shakes his head, and I don't miss the bitter tone in her voice. "She told me one night, the night I proposed, that we should see other people. Cass broke my heart." After tossing a couple of twenties on the table, he stands and stuffs the wallet in his pocket.

I can see his distress as he storms quickly from the table. Once I bounce out of the booth, I chase after him.

"I didn't mean to be nosy, Trent. If she broke your heart, why do you carry her around in your pocket every day?" I question.

He doesn't answer until he's emerged from the restaurant. "Because I just can, okay? I loved her. When she left me, it was so random. She crushed me."

Tears fill my eyes for him. That woman truly broke him.

"Why didn't you go after her?"

A sigh rushes from him and his shoulders slump. "I don't know. My pride got in the way."

Upon walking over to him, I envelop him in a hug. The hug is nothing but a friend comforting a friend. "I'm sorry. You'll find love again."

With a soft sweep of his hand along the hair hanging down my back, he whispers, "Thank you. I'm glad that you found it."

Is he right?

Do I love Thad?

Thad is normally panty-melting hot, but tonight, he's panty-*exploding* hot. The man looks sexy and dangerous wearing his black formalwear. His normally disheveled hair has been gelled into a style that just begs to be messed up. I love how I can see one of the tiger claws barely peeking out above the collar. Because, even though he's conforming to the rules of the dress code, he is deep down a rebel—my rebel.

"Have I told you how fucking beautiful you are?" Thad asks for about the ninth time since he picked me up for the benefit.

I borrowed one of Andi's cocktail dresses—a cream-colored, sleeveless, form-fitting dress that is floor length. It cinches on the left side of my waist and is adorned with pearls and rhinestones. She'd suggested this dress first, but I didn't agree on it—even though it was my favorite—because I wanted to try on all of her other dresses first. That woman has more clothes than Jackson has Harry Potter memorabilia. Walking into her closet is a million times better than any store in New York City. She's a few inches shorter than I am, but this dress works because I'm wearing low heels, whereas she wore it with four-inch hooker heels.

"I think you mentioned it once," I tease and lean over to peck his cheek. "You're pretty hot yourself."

His scruff is beginning to grow out again, and I clench the muscles of my sex as we walk, forcing away the thought of his prickly cheeks scratching the inner parts of my thighs as he tastes me.

He stops before we enter the banquet hall of the hotel. "You're so fucking hot, woman. You're like my very own Oreo—dark-chocolate goodness on the outside with a creamy, delicious-as-fuck center. Maybe we should bail and let me have a bite," he growls and dips his lips to my exposed neck.

Whatever was upsetting him earlier has seemed to disappear. He seems drunk, but not from any alcohol—he's drunk on me. I'm not complaining one bit about the needful way he gently sucks on my neck.

"Ah," I moan softly. "You might have to bite several times to make sure I taste good."

His hands slide around my ass and he jerks me to him. My nipples have hardened and feel sensitive as the material of my dress scratches them. Unfortunately, a voice douses our moment in ice water.

"Thaddeus darling, what did I say about not embarrassing me? Making out with your girlfriend in public would fall into the category of embarrassing things," Dr. Sutton coldly snaps from behind us.

When my eyes reluctantly find hers, she glares at me.

"Oh, it's you again. I see you're fast making your way through my family. Stay away from my husband."

I blink several times in shock. Thad's entire body tenses and he whirls around. I know he's dead set on defending my honor, but she's already stepped inside of the event and into the crowd of people.

"Fuck. I'm so sorry, O. You didn't deserve that," he growls as he turns back to look at me.

I shake away her nastiness and stand on my tiptoes to kiss his nose. "It's okay. Remember, my mom is just like her. I can handle it."

His hands skim up to my neck and he slips his thumbs under my chin, lifting my face to his. I nearly melt under his heated gaze. God, this man does *things* to me. He dips his lips to mine and kisses me so deeply that my knees wobble. If we were at my place, I'd let him do things to my body—very, dirty things. His phone rings in his pocket, startling the both of us, and he tenses. I was going to be a naughty girl and feel him up as I retrieved it from his pants pocket, but the moment my hand slips in, he tightly grips my wrist.

"Don't."

I don't fight him when he pulls my hand back out and steps away from me. Something is going on. I knew it.

"Who is that?" I demand.

He shakes his head in frustration. "It's nobody."

"It's somebody, Thad. Don't bullshit me. Ever since this morning, you've been acting strange. You haven't taken anything, have you? You don't plan on taking anything, do you?" My voice has risen a few octaves. I hate myself for even accusing him of doing drugs, but I don't understand his sudden change in behavior.

Last night, we went to bed perfectly happy and feeling closer than ever before. And for some reason, this morning, he bailed on me and has been acting weird ever since.

"It's nothing."

I place my hands on my hips and glare at him. "Then show me."

He sighs but pulls out his phone and holds it up to me. Missed call and voicemail from Kurt. Kurt, his best friend—Kurt, his provider of drugs.

"Play the voicemail. If it were nothing, you wouldn't be behaving so strangely. Are you sure you aren't doing drugs? Did you go to Kurt's this morning?"

He flinches and looks down at the floor. His eyes stay there as he answers me with a tone that I can tell is a lie. "No, I'm not doing drugs, and I didn't go to Kurt's this *morning*."

"Then play the voicemail." My voice is quiet. I won't feel better until I've made sure he didn't take any drugs. If he did, we'll proceed from there.

"Please don't make me do this, O." Pure desperation. He *did* do drugs.

I hold my palm out and he reluctantly drops it into my hand. His eyes are panicked but resigned. With a final frustrated sigh, he crosses his arms across his chest and takes a few steps away from me. I hit play just as I see Trent striding toward us.

"Hey, man," Kurt's voice rasps out. He sounds hungover and tired. "Thanks for coming over last night. Whitney wanted me to thank you for taking care of her in the shower." He continues rambling on about hanging out again, no pressure, blah-blah-bah. All I heard was 'ex-girlfriend' and 'shower.'

"You left my bed in the middle of the night to go fuck Whitney?" I hiss out at Thad.

He whirls around and stalks over to me. "O!" He reaches out and seizes my bare bicep. I try to shake him off, but he tightens his grip so I won't get away. "It's not what you think."

"Then what is it, Thad? Tell me, because right now, it sounds pretty damn awful!"

He drops his head shamefully but doesn't answer me.

"Let go of me. I need to get away from you right now," I grumble and once again try to free myself from his grasp.

When he doesn't let go of me, I slap his face. I don't slap it hard, but I do slap him hard enough to get his attention. However, he's unrelenting and stays in his position. Even though I'm pissed at him, his gaze melts me with the way he is furiously glaring down at me. The flesh on my chest burns at his proximity and I curse my traitorous body—the same body that seems to forgive him before my head does.

"Let her go, Thad," Trent's snarls from beside me. In my fury, I didn't notice his arrival.

Thad snaps his attention over to Trent. "Fuck you, brother. She's my woman and I need to talk to her."

"Thad," Trent growls out in warning.

When he doesn't release me, Trent hauls back and socks Thad in the stomach, sending him flying backwards.

"Into the bathroom. Now," a cold voice hisses from behind us.

We all look over to see a furious Dr. Sutton pointing to the men's bathroom.

Can this evening get any fucking worse?

As I meet Dr. Sutton's evil glare, I know that, in fact, it can.

"What is going on with the three of you?" she snarls once we're safe inside the bathroom, away from prying eyes.

"Nothing," Thad and I answer at the same time.

I don't miss the twitch of a smile on his lips. We can fix this—*hopefully*.

"Don't 'nothing' me. You and your brother were having a grade school brawl in the lobby of my benefit!" she snaps at Thad.

His shoulders straighten and he meets her evil stare with one of his own.

"What happened?" she demands again, taking her turn to look each of us in the eye.

Trent shrugs his shoulders, and I'm shocked that he hasn't ratted us out.

My eyes find Thad's—I see the remorse as he regards me. What really happened last night? I wish we were alone so he could tell me the story. If he slept with her, I'll be heartbroken.

Just like he was when you slept with his brother.

I bite my lip and try to ignore the sting of my heart. He and I really need to talk.

"You're nothing but trouble," she grumbles to Thad.

We both flinch at her hateful words.

"From the day I had to pick you up from the second grade for fighting, I knew it. You've been nothing but one difficulty after the other ever since."

Thad throws his hands up in the air, "You're a real piece of work, Mother. O, I'm sorry." He turns on his heel and storms out of the bathroom.

When I turn to go after him, sharp claws dig into my arm.

"Not so fast, little girl." Her words drip with disgust.

I turn and look into the eyes of the woman who has hated my guts since day one. "Let me go, lady."

She narrows her eyes at me.

"Mother, that's enough," Trent growls at her.

I have trouble masking my shock at the fact that he spoke up against her.

She laughs disdainfully. "See, this is the problem, son. This devilish woman has weaseled her way into our lives and has my own son acting out against me. She's nothing but a trampy jezebel that thrives on ripping families apart."

I jerk from her grip and am about to lay into the woman when someone emerges from one of the bathroom stalls.

Dr. Ellis.

"Martin, I'm so sorry you had to overhear our family heart-to-heart," she purrs in a sugary tone.

She knows him?

"It didn't sound like a heart-to-heart to me, Evette," he snips out. "In fact, it sounded like an attack on Opal."

Evette. They most certainly know each other.

"I'm sorry, Martin, but this brat has done nothing but shake things up in my family since she showed up with my son."

He walks over to me and slides his arm around me. "You okay, kid?" he whispers as he hugs me tight from the side.

I nod as I attempt to not shed a tear for this woman—the woman who is now gaping at our friendly exchange.

"She's not a brat—she's my daughter. And I think you owe her an apology."

A surprised rush of breath echoes in the bathroom. Was it mine? Dr. Sutton's?

"What?" I gasp and turn in his arms to look at him.

He grins down at me. "I'm sorry. I opened the results. You're mine, kid."

The emotion rippling through my veins is thick, and tears run out of my eyes as I squeeze him hard, pressing my cheek against his shoulder.

"You're my dad." I never thought I would say those words, ever. Especially not to someone who I had actually hoped was my father.

"I am—and I'm not going anywhere."

His words fill my heart. I can't wait to tell Thad. My heart sinks when I realize that he left—he's alone. I need to see him.

"Well, Evette?" He turns and looks at Dr. Sutton expectantly.

She eyes him, openmouthed, but straightens her shoulders. I glance over at Trent, and he winks at me supportively.

"I'm sorry. Now, if you'll excuse me," she mutters and bolts from the bathroom.

"How do you know her?" I ask my dad—*God, that feels weird*—in confusion after the door slams shut.

"She's my partner at the fertility practice. I've known her since med school. We've been friends for a long time, but I won't stand for her treating you badly."

I'm shocked but just nod dumbly.

"The party's waiting on us, so I need to get in there and make my speech. I'll find you afterwards and we can talk," he promises and plants a kiss on the top of my head.

"I'd like that, *Dad*." The word feels foreign on my tongue, but my heart expands in my chest.

His kind smile gets impossibly larger. "I'd like that too, *daughter*."

We both chuckle.

After another quick hug, he leaves me in the men's bathroom with Trent.

"We have to find him," I tell him softly.

His guilty eyes tell me that he agrees. With a hint of determination and an even bigger hint of love in his voice, he murmurs, "Let's go find my brother."

Chapter
TWENTY-THREE

Thad

I've lost her.

Fucking lost her.

I look down at my phone at the picture we took not even an hour ago in her apartment. She's so beautiful and looks incredibly happy in the picture. I want to make her happy forever. My heart clenches painfully from knowing that she's drawn the worst possible conclusions.

So tell her already. Fix this.

Would she even want to hear me out? Of course she would. It's Opal—bighearted, sweet, loving Opal. She'll listen. She has to listen.

I stand from the chair beside the open bar. I've spent the last ten minutes staring at the bottle of Jack Daniel's behind the bar. If given the chance to drink or have Opal in my arms, I'd choose her every time. Just like now.

I.

Choose.

Her.

Bursting from my chair, resolved on fixing things between us, I scan the banquet hall for the tall, chocolate-skinned, leggy beauty.

174

She's mine.

Everything about her is perfect. Her hair always feels so soft within my fingers, and I love tangling them in it so that she can't escape my lips when I kiss her. I love the way she smells like lavender. The scent is intoxicating—*in a healthy way*—and I can't get enough of her. She soothes my very being just by being her.

You're my person.

Her words from last night saturate my soul. She's my person too. I've never had someone who cares so deeply for me the way she does. I can see it in her eyes. She wants my happiness just as much as she wants her own. Lucky for us, our happiness is found together. We may have had a rocky start, but I know it will be worth every struggle in the end.

How will I tell her? How will I explain that I showered with my ex? I was trying to help her. Please, God, I hope she understands.

The air in the room warms several degrees just like it always does when she's in my presence. My eyes scan the room once more until I find her.

Her.

Opal.

Her back is turned to me. Long, dark hair cascades down her back nearly to her ass. And, oh, what a glorious ass it is! The silky fabric perfectly hugs the swell of her bottom. Tonight, if I can get her to forgive me, I'll make everything up to her with my mouth. I'll slide the fabric up her long, toned legs and take her in that sexy-ass dress. She'll moan my name as I drive into her. Her tits will pop out of the top of the dress when I drag it down with my fingers, and I'll worship those breasts for hours.

She's my drug.

She's also my recovery.

She's my person.

I'm mentally forcing my cock back into submission so I can claim my woman when a familiar, suited man steps beside her.

Trent.

She's mine!

As if on cue, he slips a palm onto the small of her back and dips down to say something to her. Then she shrugs her shoulders.

175

Is she so quick to leave me for him? The moment I walk out the door, she takes comfort in the first warm body? The warm body of my brother?

My entire body tenses and I drag my eyes back over to the bar.

Fuck!

When I turn back to look in her direction, I see her pointing right at me. I sadly shake my head. Get me out of this fucking room already. Stalking over to the bar, I reach over and yank the bottle of Jack right off the counter.

"What the h—" the bartender starts, but I wave him off.

"Put it on Evette Sutton's tab," I snap as I storm out of the banquet hall.

I have to fucking get out of here. There's no way in hell I can watch him—*my own fucking brother*—comfort my woman.

My woman.

So why am I running away from her?

I try to will myself to stop, but my legs just go and go until I find myself in my car. I don't make any moves to turn on the vehicle. I just sit.

Alone.

I pick up the bottle and raise it.

One drink.

Just one.

It will take the edge off.

I twist off the cap and bring the opening to my nose. The smell is familiar, and my chest tightens with need. Will the compulsion always be there? Will these vices always have a claim on my soul?

I inhale it again and close my eyes.

Just one drink. *Just one.*

Parting my lips, I imagine the amber liquid burning my tongue as I taste it. With each pretend swish of the alcohol in my mouth, my throat burns, practically begs to swallow it. But I don't sip the liquid.

Instead, I calmly screw the cap back on.

Opal.

She wins every time. This alcohol does nothing to soothe the ache in my heart. The only one with those powers is nearly six feet tall and a damn knockout.

She's mine.

Then go get her!

After wrenching the car door open, I stand and glare at the wall of the parking garage. Then my gaze falls to the bottle of Jack that I have clenched tight in my grasp.

Fuck this disease. I'm going after my woman.

In a dramatic move, I sling the bottle at the wall and watch it explode all over it. Glass litters the ground below and the dark liquid runs down the concrete.

Take that, Mom.

Take that, Jack.

"I'm proud of you." *Her voice.*

Turning around, I see my woman, my Opal, standing before me with a beautiful smile on her face. *She's proud.* And it fucking shows.

"We'll make this work, Thad," she says softly as she approaches me. "Whatever happened, we'll fix it. I'll fight for you—just like Olive fought for Bray. You're my person."

I groan when her hands find my chest and slide up to my neck.

Lavender.

Intoxicating.

Opal.

Inhaling her, I close my eyes and wrap my arms around her, hugging her to me. When I reopen them, I see Trent beaming at me from near the elevators. He nods in approval and gives me a thumbs-up before disappearing inside.

A misunderstanding. *A mistake.*

"I'm sorry, O," I whisper into her hair. "I just went over there to help them. Kurt's my best friend, and when he called in the middle of the night saying Whitney needed help, I couldn't just ignore it. Nothing happened with Whit—I just bathed her and made sure she was okay. I didn't use any drugs."

She sniffles and tilts her head up to look at me. "I'm an awful person. I knew deep down you didn't—I just knew. I'm sorry I accused you. Please forgive me."

My eyes search her melted-chocolate ones. Love shines there. And it feels fucking amazing to be seen in someone's eyes like that. In *her* eyes.

"You're my person too, you know. I fight for you every day. But with me, I fight the demons—because you're worth it, O. You'll always be worth it. I'll slay any dragon to be with you." I kiss her softly on the lips.

"My knight in shining armor," she giggles.

I nip at her bottom lip with my teeth and she whimpers. "I'll lock you in the tower and ravish your body forever, my queen." Then my tongue darts out and I taste her in a brief kiss.

She tastes so fucking delicious.

"Sounds like the perfect fairytale ending," she manages between kisses. "When do we get this party started?"

I slide my hands down her silky dress and cup her tight ass. "It starts the moment I get to fuck you in this dress."

She pulls away and cocks an eyebrow at me. With a wave of her hand to my car, she grins saucily at me. "Our chariot awaits, lover boy. I'm ready for my happily ever after."

Her squeal echoes through the parking garage when I pick her up and heave her over my shoulder.

I show her a happy ending over and over in the back seat of my Dad's Lexus.

Chapter TWENTY-FOUR

Opal

"Congratulations, little sister," Olive smiles and hugs me proudly.

When she releases me, she walks over to where my dad's laughing with Bray, Thad, and Trent. Abby's sitting like a princess on her daddy's shoulders. I love all of them.

My happy ever after.

Life is *almost* perfect.

As my eyes scan the crowd, I can't help the disappointment that courses through my veins. In a perfect world, she'd have come to see me walk across that stage.

This isn't a perfect world.

"Black is a good color on you. Makes you seem taller."

I freeze. Her voice. She's here.

Spinning around, I'm shocked to see my mother standing primly, wearing a floral-print dress and matching hat. She doesn't smile—no surprise there—but I see a flicker of pride.

"Momma, you came."

She waves her hand as if it's no big deal. "You bought the tickets and reserved a hotel room. It would have been rude not to."

My heart sinks.

"Maybe you came because you truly love her and have a terrible way of showing it," a deep voice says from behind me.

The warm, heavy arm of my father tucks me into him in a supportive embrace. He and I have made up for lost time in the past couple of weeks. We've spent a lot of lunches and evenings together. And Dr. Sutton has even tried to save face and had us all over a couple of times for dinner. I've been happy.

My mother's eyes widen as she sees my father for the first time in a long time.

"You're still as beautiful as the day I met you, Yolanda. What happened to your heart? What made you shut your children out?" He whispers his questions softly—clearly wanting to give her the benefit of the doubt. He still loves her, even after all these years.

"Martin." Momma murmurs his name and it is thick with emotion as she greedily devours the appearance of my father.

He leans down and kisses the top of my head. When he reaches for her, she doesn't flinch. Instead, she leans toward him, which confuses me. I've never seen anything but regret and annoyance flow through her veins. Seeing her draw closer to him as if he's a magnet is baffling.

"I've missed you, Yo-Yo."

Yo-Yo?

A sob escapes her.

Her voice is shaky when she speaks. "She has your eyes, Marty. Every time I look at her, I see you. Your eyes, through her, begged me to find you—to love you. I'm so sorry." Her apology is directed at me. "And Olive. For years, she asked about you. Years. It was too much. My heart was broken, completely and utterly broken. I'm so sorry." This time, it's directed at him.

"Grandpa? Who is this?" Abby's chipmunk voice warms my soul.

The moment I reintroduced Olive to Martin, Abby took to calling him her grandpa. It stuck and nobody ever corrected her. He chuckles and sends her a loving glance.

One day, a long time ago, my father made a mistake. He made the mistake of falling for my mother and Olive. But it was a mistake he saw as a blessing.

And as I look at the way my mother looks at him—as if he hung the moon—I suddenly have hope. The guilt in her eyes is visible as tears fill them. And when they flit up to mine, I see it—*the regret.* Regret of how she's been our entire lives. Sad thing is, I've seen the look before. I just didn't understand it. My mother's heart bled for someone our entire lives. Olive and I were a constant reminder—I was especially. We were the reminder of the biggest mistake of her life.

That mistake wasn't me.

I finally see that.

Her mistake was leaving. She broke her own heart.

"That's your Grandma Yo-Yo," Dad smiles down at her. He's the glue. He's always been the glue.

"I love yo-yos, Grandma. So that means I love you!" Abby informs her with a squeal. That Abby will melt anyone's heart—even the heart of an ice queen.

Momma sobs loudly when Abby wraps her tiny arms around her waist.

"I told you that you'd love her," Olive says knowingly to our mother as she comes to stand beside me.

My mother just nods. She knows. Life will never be the same for her again.

"I'm so sorry, girls." Her arms open, and so does my heart.

Olive and I don't walk. We don't hesitate—we *run* into her arms. The three of us sob as she begs us for our forgiveness.

She made a mistake. We all make them. Everyone deserves a chance at redemption.

"I'm so sorry. I'm so sorry." Her new mantra. Over and over.

I feel the comforting arms of my father as he hugs the three of us to him. Large, protective arms. The arms of a father. Our glue.

"Why don't you guys go on to Evette's? We'll be by later. Your mother and I need to catch up. *Alone.*"

Olive and I giggle as we pull away. We know what sort of catching up they'll be doing. The very idea of my father and mother kissing, *among other things*, should be disturbing, but it's not. I crave their happiness just as much as I do my own. After almost twenty-three years, we can finally be a family.

No more mistakes. Only happiness.

"I'm proud of you." Thad smiles and kisses the top of my head as we walk in the front door. Ever since the first night we came over to Thad and Trent's parents' for dinner with my dad, he shook things up. He called Evette out on her formalities.

"Why are we knocking?" Dad asks as we stand at Evette's front door.

My palms are sweaty with nerves. Tonight is the first night I've seen her since she accused me of trying to wreck her family in the bathroom of the benefit. I'm anxious but feel protected from her wicked ways between my father and Thad.

"She's very formal," Thad finally answers. He's embarrassed. All he's ever wanted is for acceptance from his mother. The night we reunited at the benefit, he packed his bags and has been staying with me until the place he's looking at pans out.

"Formal? This is insane." Dad reaches for the knob and walks right on in without waiting for an answer.

Thad and I eye each other widely.

"Evette," Dad booms once we walk into the entryway.

It still freaks me out that he talks to her so boldly. But, after having been partners and friends for decades, I guess he's earned that right.

"Martin, so good to see you," she purrs in her familiar tone.

He ignores her greeting and cuts straight to the chase. "Family is always welcome, Evette. My mother always had her door open for me. That's what a parent does for their child—they take care of them. Always."

Walking past her, he makes his way into the parlor to shake hands with TS. Thad and I stare at Dr. Sutton in shock.

Her mouth opens and closes a few times. Finally, she speaks. "Thaddeus, you have a key. Use it next time."

That woman is a bitch. But that is progress. Thad and I exchange a hopeful glance. My dad is special.

God, I love him.

He turns the knob and we walk inside. Trent left graduation before we did, so he's already standing in the entryway when we get there. Olive and Bray took Abby home since it was getting late.

"Congrats, Opal. You did well," he beams and hands me a bouquet of lilies.

Thad's hand finds mine and squeezes it possessively. Even though he knows that Trent is not a threat to our relationship, he still has some deep-seated, manly instinct to protect me. It secretly turns me on that, at a moment's notice, he'll toss me over his shoulder 'caveman style' and fuck me into tomorrow just to stake his claim.

"Thanks, Trent. These are beautiful," I grin as we follow him into the parlor.

TS sits in his usual spot, his iPad in his lap. Trent sits beside him and they start chatting animatedly about some trending mutual funds.

"Opal. Thad." Dr. Sutton's smile is strained, but she appears to be trying. "Marie is almost finished with dessert. Here. Let me cut the ends off those and put them in some water."

I hand her the flowers and watch her hurry from the room. Her demeanor changed the moment Dad made her apologize to me. I can see that she knows that what she did was wrong—even if she'll never admit it. She's still incredibly uncomfortable in my presence.

When we hear the front door open, I smile. Dad and Momma must be here to join us. I guess old-people make-out sessions don't last long. When my dad steps into the doorway of the parlor, I start toward him in greeting.

And then my smile falls and my feet freeze.

The tall, solid, black man standing in the parlor doorway is *not* my father.

Drake.

By the time Thad realizes who it is, Drake already has a gun raised and trained on me. "Don't move or she's taking a bullet to the head, motherfucker."

My eyes fly to Trent and TS. Both men have tensed but are frozen in fear. One wrong move and Drake will paint Dr. Sutton's perfect home with my blood.

How is this even happening? How is my happy ending going to end up as a nightmare?

"Drake," I whimper.

His finger tightens around the trigger, but he doesn't squeeze. Yet.

"Four years, Opal. You put me away for four years. Did you really think I wouldn't come back for you? For your sister? For my little girl?" he snarls.

My heart flares to life. I remember Olive telling me that he assumed Abby was his child even though they hadn't even been together when she and Bray had conceived her. The man is fucking delusional.

Thad slowly moves me behind him. "Just leave, man. Opal didn't do anything to you." His voice is a growl, low and menacing.

"Fuck you! Of course she did something—she did everything! She took away my freedom just like I took her virginity. Don't think I won't plow through you to get to her. I've got plenty of bullets, asshole. I'm taking her with me. We have catching up to do," he grumbles suggestively as his eyes skim down my bare legs, which are peeking out from under my dress.

My mind is back in the apartment. The memories of him taking me, hurting me, beating the shit out of me. A horrified sob bursts from my throat.

"Over my dead body!" Thad snaps loudly.

Drake laughs like a lunatic. "Don't mind if I do."

I'm frozen. Things play out in slow motion. My screams. Thad's preparing to shove me out of the way. TS and Trent rising from the couch.

And her.

The glint.

The scissors.

The blood.

I blink in shock and horror as Drake's blood spurts out of the side of his neck. His gun falls first and then, wide-eyed, he crumples to the floor. He tries desperately to hold his neck together, but his efforts are futile. The main artery of his neck has been severed. The artery only a doctor could pierce with perfect aim and precision.

Nobody moves to save him. We just watch him die.

When his body stops twitching and the puddle of blood stops growing, I look up at Dr. Sutton. She narrows her eyes at me, the bloody scissors remaining firmly in her grip at her side. Her gray bun is still flawless—not a hair out of place. Then her lips turn up into a smile that may haunt me in my dreams.

"Nobody messes with my family. We're Suttons and we take care of problems on our own." She raises her bloody scissors and points toward the dining room. "The crème brûlée is getting cold."

Epilogue

Thad

Four months later

"My place is ready to move in to. Are you going to miss me?" I tease Opal, who is sitting in the passenger's seat of my new truck as we drive.

After a discussion with Trent, he advised me to tap into my trust fund. He said that he'd made sure to keep it in high-paying investments while I had been refusing to use it. And because of my not ever touching it, I'd made myself a very pretty penny—a penny I'd have a hard time spending in this lifetime. With his advisement, I kept most invested but pulled out some for other *things*.

"Why can't you just stay with me? I hate this, Thad."

I grin broadly at her. But now, she frowns. I know she's assuming the worst—assuming that I'm trying to put space between us.

If she only knew. Quite the opposite.

When I pull up to the first property I started flipping, the one she helped me with, she can't hide the excitement. As soon as she eyes the "sold" sign, she squeals.

"You bought it! This is fantastic!" she exclaims and nearly falls out of the truck in her hurry to get inside.

Chuckling, I turn off the truck and follow her to the welcoming, red front door. She bounds up the three steps and stands in front of it. Then I admire her cute ass as she waits for me to join her. When I tuck the key into her back pocket, she giggles. But when she turns around to look at me, her demeanor changes.

Shocked, happy tears roll down her cheeks.

On one knee at the bottom of the steps, I look up at her with a lopsided grin. "Opal Elaine Redding, you can't go into that house. Not yet."

Her eyes widen and her hand flies to her mouth when I pull out the black velvet ring box.

"I love you, O. Honestly, I'm pretty sure I loved you the second I laid eyes on you that first night. You've been nothing but a positive, loving force in my life. Please do me the honor of marrying me. This house is ours. Our future together—if you'll have me."

She leaps down the steps and tackles me backwards. I fall onto my ass as she straddles me, raining fervent kisses all over my face. They're perfect—*she's perfect.*

"Yes, Thad! You're my person. I knew it the second I saw you. I love you too."

Her lips are on mine, and we are tasting each other like it's the first time. Every time is new and addicting for us.

"You're my person too, O. Always."

The house is fully furnished. Every single item, Opal had a hand in choosing—even down to the big, plush down comforter we're now lying on in *our* bed.

"How long will it take to christen every single room in this house?" she asks with sly grin.

It's only been a few minutes since we made love and my cock is already hard again—eager to be inside her.

"Eight hours tops," I tease and peck her lips.

She sighs, and I watch her gaze skitter around the room as she admires our handiwork. "If only my eight-hour workday was that fun..." her voice trails off.

I know that, ever since she took the position in the payroll department at Compton Enterprises, she's been unhappy. She told me that, each day, she actually watches the clock on the wall slowly tick by.

Rolling off her, I climb from the bed and saunter over to my jeans, which are in a heap on the floor. After I retrieve my wallet, I look at her with a wicked grin. She knows what it means when I get my wallet. I wink at her as I slide out a condom and toss it at her. But as she tears the wrapper, I also take out something I know she'll appreciate.

"This is yours if you want it," I tell her as I walk back over to her.

She eyes my hand with interest. When I open my palms, she hesitantly takes the business card from my hand.

Sutton Renovation, LLC

O. Sutton – Interior Designer

"What is this?" she gasps. Her voice has an excited edge to it. She's hopeful.

I take her hand and dip down to a knee in front of her. Then I softly kiss the top of her hand. "It's your happy ever after, my queen."

She pulls me up to her onto the bed and I pounce on her, nipping the flesh on her neck as I cover her body with mine. We skip the condom this time, and I enter her quickly.

"You're my happy ever after, Thad."

I'm her favorite mistake.

It actually takes us a day and a half to properly christen the house—some rooms we had to do it in several times, just to make sure. The best thing about a happily ever after is...

It is never THE END.

Crushed—A Novella

More from Andi and Jackson coming soon….

Jackson

My wife is dying.

With every breath she takes, every second that passes, she dies a little more. I can hardly stand to watch it. I'm not callous or unloving—quite the opposite, actually. I love her so much that I want to kick the fucking machine that the doctor is using to assess her because I can't stand seeing her this way. I want to storm from this room and punch anyone who even looks at me the wrong way in the teeth because they don't understand how it feels to slowly lose the one they love.

And I am losing her.

Little by little.

Life just isn't fair.

As if clued in to my melancholy thoughts, she squeezes my hand from the bed. I glance briefly at the monitor and then my eyes land on hers. They're the saddest fucking eyes on the planet, and they gut me.

I can't fucking do this anymore.

"I need a drink of water," I grumble under my breath to her. I'll do anything to get out of this room.

"Jackson, don't be nervous. Just sit tight. Everything will be okay, babe." Her words are soft and reassuring.

Why the fuck is she reassuring me? What kind of asshole am I? I'm the one who needs to take my fucking panties off and be a man, to reassure my wife—not the other way around.

I lean down and kiss her forehead. I can't lose her. I just can't.

"I'm sorry." My voice is nearly inaudible. But my Andi hears—she always hears.

The doctor clears his throat and he smiles at me—fucking smiles. Maybe I should throttle his ass. After all, he's an accomplice in this slow death of hers. My free hand clenches into a fist.

She squeezes my hand once again and my anger melts a bit. With a sigh, I dip down and press a kiss to her soft lips. Why can't I just fix it? All of it?

"You see it? Right there?" the doctor asks with a gentle smile.

Andi's eyes fill with tears and her hand is shaking in mine. When she turns to look at me, I'm almost torn in two by her expression.

The hope in her eyes fucking cuts me to my core.

"Three?" she chokes out on a sob.

Does God really answer prayers? Right now, he's taunting me, ignoring my pleas.

"Yep, three. Congratulations, Mrs. Compton. You're pregnant."

The excited chatter of my wife is muted as the room spins around me. Where Andi has hope, dread fills every ounce of my being. In that single moment in the doctor's office, I know.

I know without a shadow of a doubt.

This pregnancy will kill my wife.

A sneak peek into Trent's story—coming soon in 2015!

Trent

I stare at the piece of paper in my hand that mocks me.

This sort of thing just doesn't happen to people like me. I'm the Golden Child. The man with no speeding tickets and zero cavities at every dentist visit. I help old ladies cross the street. People call on me to help them out of financial trouble.

I'm good. *The best, even.*

Squeezing my eyes shut, I lean back in my office chair.

What will my mother think?

Just imagining making that phone call sends panic through my veins.

I peek my eyes open and glance back down at the document—the very official document.

Cassidy.

My attorney, Calvin, faxed over this birth certificate on his way out of the office. He should be here soon to discuss it. But for the past twenty minutes, I've been staring at it. There has to be some mistake.

I'm not a father. Not the father of some almost four-year-old little boy. It's impossible.

You had unprotected sex that one night—the night before you proposed—the night before she turned you down.

People don't get pregnant after one time of unprotected sex. This cannot be happening.

A soft knock on my office door drags my attention from the birth certificate.

"Come in," I command hoarsely. I hate the shakiness in my voice.

A thought suddenly takes root in my mind. She'll want me back. If we have a kid together, she'll have to want me back. We could be a family.

Hope threads itself through my heart as Calvin walks in. His downcast eyes immediately put my nerves on edge.

"I'll take the paternity test. If the kid is mine, I want to do what's right." It's the truth. I'll do it for her. *For Cassidy.*

Calvin sighs and slides another very official document across my

191

desk.

Tears blur my vision.

No.

A death certificate.

Cassidy Francine Thomas.

Thirty-one years old.

Dead.

He begins rattling off information, but the roar in my head is too much. She can't be dead. Cassidy was a normal, healthy woman. This doesn't make sense.

"Did you hear me?" he demands loudly.

My tear-stained eyes find his in question.

"Social services will be by tomorrow morning. You're the father on the birth certificate," he says softly. "Tomorrow, they are bringing you your son."

My son.

Cassidy is dead and I have a son.

Letters FROM STADIL

by ANNE JOLIN & K WEBSTER

Daulton

"END OF THE ROAD, BUDDY," the stranger grumbles, startling me from my thoughts.

If only he knew. It truly is the end of the road. Not in an awful 'my life is ending' sort of way. But more of an 'I'm now an adult, so fun times are over' way. In a couple of weeks, I'll be right back home, following in my father's footsteps and embarking on a career as an attorney at his firm.

I look over at the old man with the salt-and-pepper stubble scattered all over his face. "I appreciate the ride. Do you know where I can stay around here?"

He chuckles and it reminds me of my grandfather. "Best place around these parts is The Saltvand Rose. It's a quaint little B&B at the end of Nordentoft gode. I'll warn you though. They'll put you to work. But a strapping young man like yourself won't mind. Tell them Jesper sent you." He's pointing straight ahead, so I assume that's the direction I should head.

"Thanks again for the ride." I try to hand him a wad full of kroner for his help, but he waves it away.

"The company was thanks enough. I ride back in to Copenhagen on Sundays, so when you're ready to head back, have Soren ring me and I'll pick you up."

I don't stick around to ask who Soren is. Instead, I slide out of the truck and retrieve my backpack from the bed. After a quick wave, I turn and take in the breathtaking view. The ride from Copenhagen was long and hot in the truck with no air conditioning. The North Sea is calling out to me with each crashing wave, so I kick off my flip-flops and pick them up before trudging through the sand towards the water.

This summer has been the best ever. After graduating from law school, I took a much-needed break to backpack across Europe. Alone. My best friend, Brody, had offered to come with me, but his fiancée had thrown a bitch fit because she couldn't be away from him for two months. As disappointed as Brody had been, I'd been okay with it. I had looked forward to the isolation and inner reflection.

Denmark is the last leg of my journey. I have two weeks before I catch a plane back to New York—*back to reality*.

I look up and down along the beach and find it dead aside from a runner and someone walking a dog. The sand between my toes is relaxing as I truck my way to the edge of the water. After dropping my backpack into the sand along with my flip-flops, I toe the water to test the temperature. It's a little brisk, but I'm hot as hell, so I think I'll live. I quickly yank off my shirt and toss it with my stuff.

As I step into the water, I try to push away the anxiety that lies beneath the surface of my mind. I'm about to run with the wolves—my father being the leader of the pack. It's what I've worked tirelessly to achieve, but deep down, I wonder how fully it will satisfy me.

When the chilly water hits my hips, I suppress a shiver. It feels great to cool off and wash away the grime from my trip. I'm about to dive in and fully submerge myself when I hear high-pitched screams.

I turn my head in the direction of the sound to see the runner from earlier hauling ass down the beach toward me while frantically waving her arms in the air. My first instinct is sharks. Nervously, I glance around me and breathe a sigh of relief when I don't see any sea monsters.

"Get out of the water!" the woman calls out to me.

I pause for a moment to watch her long, blond ponytail swish from left to right as she runs. My eyes drop to her breasts, which are encased in a tight, black sports bra. With each step, they bounce beautifully. Thank God for this cold-ass water.

There doesn't seem to be any immediate threat, so I turn away from her and dip farther into the water until the coolness slides its icy fingers around my ribs.

"Do you have a death wish?" the feminine voice yells.

I turn to look at her in confusion. She now stands at the edge of the water, huffing with exertion, her tiny hands on her curvy little hips. Now that she's closer, I can really admire the view. The woman is only about five foot six, but her black yoga pants somehow make her look even taller. However, even though she's stunning as hell, I'm not one for responding well to being told what to do.

"I'm going swimming. So unless Jaws or the Loch Ness Monster is creeping around under the water, I'm not getting out."

I'm about to tell her to run along when a strong current slides around my ankle and yanks me under. Momentarily, I'm stunned, not having expected the water to be so powerful.

But swimming is my thing.

I'm built from years of competitive swimming and know what to do in these situations. Hell, I was a lifeguard every summer aside from this one since I was sixteen. I start swimming with the current, making my way toward shore. I've just pulled myself from the tentacles of the wicked current when I hear a shriek.

My heart sinks when I turn just in time to see a blond ponytail get pulled underwater.

What the fuck?

Seconds later, I see the woman resurface and begin thrashing as she fights the pull of the current. My heart speeds up as I realize we have only a few seconds of her struggling against it before it will consumer her.

"Swim with the current!" I yell to her as I start swimming toward her.

She jerks at my command, and I see her desperately attempting to do as I've told her. I push through the water until I'm near her and snatch her bicep as she rushes by. The water is violent, but I pull her hard until she's safe in my arms.

"Are you okay?" I demand as I retreat toward the safety of the shore with the slight woman in my grasp.

When she doesn't respond, I panic. Quickly, I race out of the water with her in my hold until I collapse onto the dry sand, landing on top of her. Her plump lips are slightly purple and I'm unsure if it's from sucking in a lungful of water or the cold of the ocean. I'm about to perform CPR when she coughs and spits out some seawater.

"Thank fuck you're okay," I sigh in relief. My hand, with a mind of its own, strokes a blond strand of hair out of her eye.

She blinks several times before speaking. "You saved me."

I can't stop looking at her lips as they quickly turn pinker with each passing breath. God, she's even more beautiful up close.

"I saved you as you were trying to save me. Let's leave the rescues to me. We'll leave being cute to you." I wink at her and my lips curl into a smug grin.

"Ugh. Americans," she sighs in feigned annoyance.

Every moment in my life has been calculated, routine, scheduled. But today, I feel spontaneous. Today, I want to do something that's not me.

Before I can talk myself out of it, I dip my head down to hers and softly kiss her lip—the bottom one I've been eyeing. She tastes like apples and cinnamon—like a mix of heaven and home. Just one taste and something becomes very real.

I'm already addicted to her.

Lene

MY MIND ATTEMPTS TO NEGOTIATE with me, to find a reason why kissing this stranger isn't a good idea, but it's a weak battle at best. There's something electric I've never felt before today in his kiss. I can't help but want more.

I run my hands up his bare chest, tangling my cold fingers in his dark-brown hair. His lips have warmed since our dangerous entanglement with the water, and I whimper as his tongue enters my mouth, deepening our kiss.

I feel entirely lost to reality, as if it's all a dream and it will suddenly all be gone.

"Er du okay!?"

He pulls his lips a mere inch from mine as the sound of the voice coming down the beach intrudes on our private moment. My stranger's eyes are the palest shade of green and utterly captivating as they stare into my own blue eyes. There's something there, something in his eyes. It reminds me of how a caged animal would look if suddenly set free in the wild—adventurous and uninhibited perhaps.

The pad of his thumb brushes over my bottom lip and I shiver, not entirely from the cold.

When I close my eyes as he leans down to touch his lips to mine again, I'm rewarded by a far messier kiss than I expected. My eyes spring open just as Tobias's wet tongue slaps the side of my face again.

"Er I totalt skøre?"

I turn my head to the side to find an upset Rikke glaring down at us, asking if we are totally crazy. "Han ved det ikke, Rikke," I respond, letting her know that my handsome stranger was unaware of the dangers The North Sea presents. It's beautiful but deadly, killing at least a handful of visiting tourists in the riptide every year.

Rikke's eyes skitter across our outstretched bodies on the beach before she quirks an eyebrow. I instantly blush at the thought of what we must look like: a tangled mess of wet bodies in the sand, with bruised lips and passionate eyes.

"Jeg tror ikke at han taler dansk." Rikke smirks at me, gesturing towards the man above me before calling Tobias and retreating down the beach towards her home.

I blush again, feeling rude as a peek back up into his eyes. "I'm sorry. You don't speak Danish, do you?" I ask him softly.

He chuckles, wiping a strand of hair that has escaped from my ponytail off my face. "No, darlin', I don't, but I would learn if you were teaching me." His lips curl into that heart-stopping grin again, and he leans down, covering his chest with mine.

I suddenly find it entirely too difficult to breathe as he cups my face in his left hand.

"You're beautiful. What is your name?" he asks.

"I can't…" I struggle to speak. "I can't breathe," I gasp out.

His grin widens. "Well, this is a bit cheesier than I would usually dish out on a first date, but you took my breath away the moment I saw you screaming at me down the beach," he confesses.

"No. I can't…" I try again. "You're on top of me. I can't breathe," I manage to get out, gently shoving his chest with my hands.

My stranger's eyes widen and he quickly rolls onto the beach beside me. I suck in a deep breath of air.

"I'm sorry! Are you okay?" he asks, his eyes frantically running over my body in a panic.

I smile at his concern for my wellbeing and reach out to touch his arm. "I'm perfectly fine. You're just a little heavy"—I gesture towards him—"and I think you were crushing my lungs." I laugh into the wind at the absurdity of our encounter.

He chuckles, reaching out his hand. "Daulton Bishop, the"—he smirks at me—"and I quote you here"—he rolls his eyes dramatically—"'Ugh. American.'"

I stifle a laugh again, rolling to my side and propping my head up on my elbow. "Lene Kirkegaard," I say, placing my small hand in his much larger one. "The cute Dane."

He stands up, pulling me up along with him. "Nice to, uh"—he runs a hand through his messy, brown hair—"meet you."

I smile at him. "Nice to meet you too. Where are you staying?"

"Actually, I was going to ask. You wouldn't happen to know where The Saltvand Rose bed and breakfast is, would you?"

I giggle at his mispronunciation of Saltvand, and he playfully narrows his eyes at me.

"Yes. I do imagine your Danish could use some sprucing up," I tease. "I know where it is." I point to the road across from the beach. "See the large, white building? It looks like an old dairy building." I wait for him to nod before I continue. "That's the main house. The redbrick building to the right is the bed and breakfast."

"Thank you, Lene." He runs his knuckles over my arm. "Do you think I can see you again?"

"I imagine you'll be seeing me much sooner than you'd expect," I tease him before blowing a kiss and jogging back down the beach.

Daulton

LENE.

I watch her cute little ass bounce in her tight, now-wet yoga pants as she makes her way back down the beach. Shit, that woman is mesmerizing as hell. She laughed at the fact that this is a small town and she'd probably see me around. I'm thanking my lucky stars for that fact because I'm going to stop at nothing until I have her back in my arms.

But first I need to shower and settle down for a bit. The trip here was long and tiring. And after a near drowning, which was followed by an immediate rescue mission, I'm exhausted.

I pick up my T-shirt and shake the sand from it before putting it back on. It would be nice to wash what I have in my bag considering I'm on my last clean pair of underwear. After I heave my bag over my shoulder, I don't bother putting my flip-flops back on and instead opt to hold them while I trudge my way down the beach.

Lene.

I can't get that girl out of my head. In high school and college, I pretty much landed any chick I set my sights on. Problem was that I never wanted any of them. It wasn't like I was gay or anything. There just wasn't ever a girl who "did things to me," as Brody called it.

But Lene. After just one chance encounter, my heart is pounding around in my chest like it's about to explode. It makes no sense, but I can't deny the thrill she sent through not only my body, but my heart as well.

"The beach is always washing up something worth looking at," a playful woman's voice calls out to me.

I didn't realize how far I walked, but now, I pause to admire the charming redbrick building Lene described, which I'm now standing

201

in front of.

"The Saltvand Rose?" I ask, still looking for the voice.

An older woman stands from behind a bush. She's beautiful despite her graying hair and slightly wrinkled face. When she smiles, I know without a doubt she was a head turner when she was younger.

"The one and only. We take in all the strays." She winks and I can't help but smile back at her.

"Got any room for a wanderer like me?"

She squints at me as she approaches. I flinch in surprise when she stands uncomfortably close and squeezes my bicep.

"You'll do. Are you ready to earn your keep?"

I grin as I remember the old man from the truck telling me that they'd want me to do just that. "I'm more than a pretty face," I joke and flex my muscle.

She blushes and playfully swats at me. "Soren will tan your hide for flirting with his old woman. I'm Bridgette, owner of this place."

I shake her hand and try to ignore the grumble in my belly. Unfortunately, she hears it and gasps.

"Oh, no, sir. We don't go hungry around here. Come on. I'll show you to our only vacant room at the moment. After you clean up—*because Lord you stink*—I'll fix you something to eat. Then I'll put you to work."

I immediately warm to this woman. She reminds me a lot of my nanny, Gertie.. Gertie was my mother in every since of the word. My real mother, even to this day, treats me as a possession she can show off to her hoity-toity friends.

"Lead the way, B."

She blushes again and shakes her head. "Americans are so flirty. Soren owns guns and he's not afraid to use them," she chuckles as I follow her into the building through a rickety screen door that squeaks in protest when we open it. Even though the outside is fairly plain and nondescript, the inside is stunning.

Bridgette doesn't give me much time to take in the beautifully decorated space because she hurries—much too quickly for someone of her height—down the hallway toward a flight of stairs. I have to stride to keep up with her.

Once we reach the landing to the second floor, she takes me to the fourth door at the end of the hallway. She pushes open the door and enters a quaint room with a queen-sized bed. I expect the room to be floor-to-ceiling floral print as most of the ones I've stayed in while in Europe have been. However, I'm amazed at the sheer modern feel to it.

The walls are painted a dark grey, nearly the color of the ocean, and white crown molding finishes with a clean look as it lines the ceiling. Modern pictures in simple frames scatter the walls. An antique globe sits proudly on a stack of old books on the desk in the corner. A grey duvet neatly covers the bed and a crème colored decorative pillow adorned with metal beads sits proudly at the top.

"Wow, Bridgette. This place is amazing and by far the nicest room I've had in two months," I praise.

"Oh, Hans, we have the best decorator. And get this—she works for free." Her eyes twinkle. The woman is slightly eccentric, but I already love that about her.

I walk over to the bed and toss my bag down. "Where can I shower?"

She points over to the closed door in the corner. "There's a small shower and your own private toilet in there, Hans. See you for supper at five."

Hans.

"Bridgette, I'm Daulton. Don't mind my awful American manners. I'm sorry I didn't introduce myself earlier."

She laughs and pats my shoulder as she walks toward the door to leave. "It's a good thing I like your rude American ways, Hans."

I'm about to remind her again that my name's not Hans, but she's already slipped out the door. Shaking my head, I strip down and head for the shower. After my first hot, steamy shower in weeks in a clean bathroom, I smile as I dry off. Then I wrap a towel around my waist and exit the room.

I'm shocked to see a woman rifling through my bag, her back to me. Fucking hell! I knew this place was too good to be true. Storming over to her, I yank her bicep and turn her to me, ready to unleash a slew of curse words on the thief, when recognition settles over me.

"Lene? What the hell are you doing?" I demand. As soon as I see her wide, blue eyes staring back at me, the angry fire is replaced by a smoldering heat of want.

"I was going to wash your things for you," she says simply, as if digging through someone else's bag without their knowing is a customary thing around here.

Shit, maybe it is.

I reluctantly release her arm and try not to eye her pink, pouty lips, which I know from experience taste fucking delicious.

"Where I come from, that isn't cool, Lene," I tell her firmly.

She frowns. "Where I come from, it's considered a nice, welcoming gesture. You're here, where I'm from, so I think it'd be proper for you to accept our way of doing things. I do expect an apology now."

I cock an eyebrow at her. The cute little thing sees absolutely nothing wrong with sneaking into a stranger's room and looking through their things without permission. I want to tell her that she's the crazy one, but I don't. Instead, I do something completely out of character for me, a man who's on his way to be an attorney—I concede without argument.

"You're right, Lene. I'm sorry. My clothes are in dire need of washing, so thank you."

Her eyes skitter down my bare chest, and a smile tugs at the corners of her lips. I watch her cheeks turn slightly pink. It's in this moment that I realize she's changed clothes and pulled her wet hair into a messy bun. Her navy-blue sundress hugs her curves slightly, and now, I'm embarrassed at what the sight is doing to my own body. She looks hot as hell.

Quickly, I turn my back to her. "Let me grab a few things from there and get dressed. I'll give you the rest to wash," I tell her hoarsely. I'm mentally trying to calm down a certain part of my body that seems more than eager to say hi.

I feel a small hand flutter lightly across the muscles of my upper back. The simple touch sends a current of electricity through my body.

"I'm sorry," she whispers, "I just had to touch you." She quickly removes her hand and scampers out the door, shutting it loudly behind her.

Well, hell. Now I need another shower. This time, a really cold one.

Acknowledgments

A big thanks goes out to my person, Matt Webster. My dear, sweet husband, you've been amazingly supportive when at times I made you question your sanity. I'll forever be grateful for your help in allowing me to follow my dream. You're my happy ever after.

This book wouldn't have been possible without the wonderful support and suggestions of my beta readers. Thank you Nikki Mc-Crae, Mandy Abel, Wendy Bear, Elizabeth Thiele, Dena Marie, JD aka Jill Bookfiend, Shannon Martin, Michelle Berndt, Michelle Ramirez, Lori Christenson, and Anne Jolin. You ladies rock my world!

A special thanks to all those that support me daily. Without your constant words of encouragement, I'd be lost. You know who you are.

Thanks a million to my fabulous editor, Mickey Reed. Girl, without your Word Ninja help, I'd have "special" stories. You make them the good kind of special.

Stacey Blake with Champagne Formats, you are the bomb. When technology produces nightmares and manuscripts come to you in pieces, you manage to smooth out the lines and deliver something beautiful. I can't thank you enough for that.

To all the bloggers out there, your support is amazing and I am so grateful that you take the time to share my books. You all have plenty on your plate but still find time and that rocks my world!

Readers…thank you. Thank you for taking a chance on me and my books. Without you, this becomes just a job. But because of your excitement and anticipation of my stories, I write with a full heart and an eagerness to deliver something you can truly enjoy. Your support means the world to me.

About the Author

I'm a thirty three year old self-proclaimed book nerd. Married to my husband for nearly twelve years, we enjoy spending time with our two lovely children. I enjoy dabbling in Photoshop when I'm not writing, and have designed most of my book covers.

This writing experience has been a blast and I've met some truly fabulous people along the way. I hope my readers enjoy reading my stories as much as I do writing them. I look forward to connecting with you all!

Follow Author K Webster on…
Facebook https://www.facebook.com/authorkwebster
Twitter https://twitter.com/KristiWebster
Website http://authorkwebster.com/
Instagram http://instagram.com/kristiwebster
Goodreads https://www.goodreads.com/user/show/10439773-k-webster

Made in the USA
Lexington, KY
02 April 2018